SEE ME

Dangerous Entanglements Book One

ANNE ROMAN

CHAPTER ONE

Hannah

The bright sunlight reflected off the tall gray buildings in downtown Atlanta. All around me, I could hear the sounds of the city echoing off each concrete wall as I walked past the bright red benches and towering magnolia trees that surrounded the park's interior.

A few homeless men and women lounged under the shade of the trees trying to escape what sun the buildings didn't block, but it wouldn't have mattered. It was mid-June in the south and even the mosquitoes would sweat like a whore in church.

I looked at the large square building in front of me as I paused at the crosswalk. They built the Fulton County Courthouse in the early 1900s. I couldn't imagine that the "golden age" that brought about art déco, flappers, and speakeasies built something so big, square, and ugly.

At least that's what others said. But not me. I loved the courthouse and everything it represented. When I moved to Atlanta to work as a federal agent, I felt like a small fish in a big pond. It was completely different from my country home, which was just a couple of hours outside of the city. Atlanta had bright lights, loud music, and gleaming buildings. I quickly fell in love with the people and the history of the city. It also helped that my sister had moved here for college, so that family was always close by.

Moving up the stairs, I pulled one of the heavy double doors open and stepped inside the cool interior, taking a deep breath to calm my nerves. The preliminary hearing today was important. Our agency had been working on this case for almost three years and we were finally close to putting the last remaining pieces into place to take down a huge human trafficking operation. The only thing that needed to happen was for our informant to give his testimony. Then, one by one, the cards of the Hildago Syndicate would fall.

"Special Agent Kelly." A deep voice called my name as I was leaving the security checkpoint, returning my items to my purse. I immediately recognized Special Agent David Williams, head of the Atlanta field office. David had been my partner before his promotion, and I still looked at him like a mentor and friend. He was a big man with dark skin and an easy smile. But you didn't want to get on his bad side or else you risked six foot and several inches of ex-UGA linebacker barreling down on you. David's wife Marie was the only person I'd ever seen him back down from, and she was a friend as well.

David nodded his head to follow him as I crossed over the gleaming floors, my heels clicking on the polished tile. I wasn't one for fashion or appearances, but I did have one vice, shoes. I loved shoes and sneakers, especially since I was more fond of working out and running than anything else. But on days like today, when I was about to close one of the biggest cases of my life, I always went for my Louboutin heels. The red soles gave me a boost of confidence, like perhaps I wasn't just some girl from the country playing at being a badass federal agent.

David's stride was so long and fast that I had to hurry to catch what he was saying as we headed toward the hallway that would lead us to the deposition room.

"...You did a good job on this case, Hannah, but I've had several phone calls from the District Attorney and the Mayor's office already trying to press us into postponing this deposition. The Hildago's are putting pressure on their political connections. I am worried that we are going to get steamrolled here." He had a small frown on his forehead, the only sign that he was worried.

"David, relax. This guy is solid. The evidence he gave us is airtight, and as soon as we get his testimony in, we've got them. We are finally going to nail these assholes after three years of hard work." My smile was hard and bright as I pushed open the heavy door that would lead into the meeting room where the judge and presumably a court-appointed lawyer waited for us. David hadn't been there when we'd found the shipping container full of women and children, packed in so tight that there was no way they could have even sat down. Some of them should not have tried to make the journey. They were too sick or young. When we'd finally pulled their decomposing bodies from the back of the container, the stench had been overwhelming and the haunted eyes of those forced to stand nearest to them would forever be burned into my brain.

It was a phoned-in tip that led us to the shipping yard. A concerned dockworker, not yet on the syndicates' payroll, had noticed unusual activity in a part of the port that was supposed to be shut down for quarantine. It had been the height of the pandemic and all shipping had come to a stop unless, of course, you were shipping illegal items or people. From there, it had been a matter of finding someone among the rescued immigrants who could identify anyone within the organization and begin to connect the dots.

When we'd finally found someone we could get access to, he was only too willing to flip for us. His little sister was one of the people who died on that container. It seems she hadn't gotten the treatment or care they had promised him. It had taken another full year of monitoring, collecting, and waiting for the right opportunity to strike, as the evidence-gathering didn't stop there. And now it was finally here, and I was looking forward to seeing justice served.

"Son of a bitch!" My voice echoed down the main atrium of the courthouse, causing the few remaining people in the building to pause what they were doing and stare. It was late in the afternoon now. Somewhere in the last 24 hours, our confidential source decided that he didn't want to talk and needed a lawyer. The lawyer he had retained was one of the top defense attorneys in the state, Loraine Coleman. What was supposed to have been an easy deposition had turned into an hours-long interrogation of me, my work ethic, my processes as a Special Agent, and somehow even my romantic life.

I remember the condescending tone she had taken when she said that maybe if I wasn't distracted by romantic office entanglements" I wouldn't be under suspicion of evidence tampering.

"You're something of a black widow, aren't you, Agent Kelly?" Her gaze had drifted over my features, taking in everything, including my Louboutins with a slight lip curl of disdain.

"Excuse me? What is that supposed to mean?" I knew I shouldn't have engaged with her, but I couldn't help it. I felt like years of hard work were slipping through my fingers like sand and I couldn't stop it.

"Well, it's just that every relationship you're engaged in seems to end in an," she glanced down at what I presumed were her notes on me. ", unexpected office transfer or request for reassignment. It seems like once you're done with your conquest, you are quite efficient at getting rid of the evidence."

"I'm sorry, I fail to see what my relationships have to do with my professionalism or ability to conduct myself as becoming of a Federal Agent."

"Wasn't Agent Williams recently appointed Special Agent in charge of the Atlanta Field Office?"

"Yes, and again, what does that have to do with anything?" By now I was looking at the judge, sure that he'd stop this line of questioning, as it was absurd.

"And wouldn't the position, should Agent Williams be relieved of his duties because the evidence in such a high profile and impactful case was unusable in court- go to you?"

"I mean it could go to any number of agents, but wait, are you say-"

She cut me off with a sharp "Please answer the question as I asked it, Agent Kelly."

My jaw had hurt from how hard I was clenching it as I said forcefully, "Yes, should Agent Williams be relieved of his duties, the position could go to me."

"And can you tell us again why there's a discrepancy between the evidence logs and what you turned over for discovery?"

"I told you. I don't know!"

At this point, both the judge and David had agreed that they would postpone the grand jury and indictment until the missing evidence could be investigated. I'd stalked out of the room before I did something regrettable. Like, punch the snarky bitch in her face. Now - that- would be unbecoming of a Federal Agent.

"Hannah...." David approached me slowly, his face an unreadable mask. Whatever his thoughts, he wasn't going to let anyone know until we were in private.

I pointed my finger down the hall that we had just come from. "You know damn well that was fucking bullshit, David. There is no way the evidence was stolen or tampered with. I wouldn't do that."

"I know. But I told you I had a bad feeling about this and this is what I meant. Someone doesn't want this guy to talk and until we find out what they got over on him, we can't do anything about it." He crossed his arms, a giant wall of calm in the face of my fiery rage. "But this isn't even what you should be mad about."

I paused, running my hands through my hair in frustration, and gave him a narrowed glare. "Oh, you mean I should be more pissed that she essentially proclaimed to the world that I was fucking my way through the office, to include my boss? Or that I was a lying, scheming, black widow, hell-bent on destroying the careers of my partners?"

He cocked a thick eyebrow at me, "Come on Hannah, she tried to get under your skin and it worked. No one is going to believe that crap. You're missing the bigger picture here. Someone tampered with the evidence from the raid on their office with......" He let the sentence trail off as the realization dawned.

"David, are you saying what I think?"

"Yes."

"Shit. We have a mole."

CHAPTER TWO

Hannah

"Sissy, you should have seen her. She was like a robot. Her hair was pulled back in a bun so tight I swear if she let it down, her face would have fallen off."

I was snickering, a mouth full of ice cream and a full glass of wine in my hand while sitting on the floor of my sister's living room for our traditional ice cream and movie night. Normally we met on the weekends, since we were both extremely busy with our jobs. But when she'd called me to see if I could meet tonight instead, I was only too happy to agree, especially after the day I'd just had.

Sissy, or Sybil, lived near the Georgia Tech campus where she worked in the research and development department. Her place was small, as most townhomes in this area were, but it suited her minimalist lifestyle. One large cream-colored rug and a sleek modern couch took up the majority of the floor space. There were only a few pieces of abstract art in muted colors on the walls and other than a crochet blanket our mother had made for her thrown casually over the back of the couch, there was hardly any color in the space. I figured her decorating style was reflective of her job. Nothing at all like my tiny apartment, whose style could only be referred to as "takeout container chic."

"You mean like an AI robot or the Terminator?" Sybil was sitting on the couch across from me, balancing her ice cream bowl on her lap, her wine glass placed safely on the end table next to her. "I bet she was just jealous that you had any 'romantic office entanglements' while she probably doesn't even have hope." Her nose wrinkled in slight disgust and I was mildly shocked at her supportive statement. Sybil normally didn't approve of my dating choices.

"But seriously, Hans, you should probably try to date outside of the office pool for a while. You know, meet a nice -normal- guy that maybe doesn't like to brag about the caliber size of his weapon or how much more he can bench press than you." And there was the dig. She went back to eating her ice cream with delicate little bites that were just so, Sybil. I watched her contemplatively and wondered, not for the first time, if we came from the same parents. Sybil was only ten months and some change younger than me, making us Irish twins. We even looked enough alike that we were often mistaken for real twins. But other than the same dark hair, green eyes, and overall features, we were complete opposites.

Our mother liked to say we were two different flavors of the same dish. I was the savory, Sissy was the sweet. Food references were Mama Kelly's favorite way of describing just about anything in life. In our mother's opinion, if food couldn't solve a problem, then nothing could.

I shrugged, getting back to her judgment over my love life choices. She was probably right. My office romance life was nothing to write a script over, but apparently, it had been enough to fuel the nasty little black widow rumor. And as soon as I found who had been feeding that bullshit to miss ice queen lawyer, they'd see just how deadly I could be.

"Enough of my office drama. What's going on with Mr. Tall, Dark & Foreign? I thought you guys were glued to each other. I half expected you to tell me he was whisking you away on some grand European vacation and that you'd see me next fall." Sybil had recently begun dating a visiting professor from some posh-sounding university in Europe.

For the past several weeks, she had apologized for canceling our regular ice cream date because her new boyfriend had plans or there was some lecture he wanted her to attend with him. It sounded dull, but I guess when a guy with an ascot and an accent asks you to "do him the honor of accompanying him" to some gala, it's hard to say, "No thanks! I need to go hang out with my sister in her ratty apartment, eating our weight in ice cream and drinking cheap wine." Not that I'd ever seen the guy to know if he actually wore an ascot. But in my opinion, he sounded like a typical stuffy European bore, so ascot it was.

Was I a little jealous that this mystery man was taking up so much of my sister's time? Maybe, just a little, but more than that, I was curious about him. It was also why I'd agreed to come to meet her at her place. I didn't want her canceling on me again. We may have been opposites, but Sybil was my best friend, and I had missed her.

"Actually," she sat up and placed her bowl of ice cream carefully next to the wineglass on her side table, "That's pretty close to what I was going to say."

"No way! I was only kidding. You're really not leaving with him, are you?" I forgot my wine and ice cream on the floor next to me as I moved to sit on my knees, facing her directly. This was huge. Not only did my sister never talk about her love life, but she'd also never appeared to be so serious about someone so quickly.

"Are you ready for that? I mean, you've only been dating for a few weeks, now you want to go on a European vacation with him?" I couldn't help it. All the dangerous scenarios began running through my mind, a bad habit from my work. Some of my fears must have bled out into my expression, because she rolled her eyes and waved her hand dismissively.

"Hannah, stop. It's not like that. There's a major convention happening and we're attending some lectures, is all. He's already there, in fact. I'm supposed to meet him." She leaned over to reach past me and picked up my wineglass, probably concerned I'd flail around and knock it over. Wine stains on her pristine rug would definitely clash. "I'm leaving tomorrow."

My mouth gaped open in shock.

"Tomorrow? Are you kidding me? Sybil, have you even told Mom and Dad? Where are you going? How long will you be gone?" I was standing now and pacing. Sure, my sister was a grown woman and only a few months younger than me, but I took my role as the oldest seriously and the idea of her going so far away made me feel overly protective.

She stood as well and crossed her arms under her chest in what I could only describe as a classic Sybil pose. "Um, actually, Hannah," she emphasized my name with a roll of her eyes, "I told mom and dad earlier this week when I went to have dinner with them." That made me stop my pacing.

"Wait, you saw mom and dad?" Sybil never went to see our parents. I wasn't sure if it was just another difference between us, or if she was just that busy with her job. But I tried to go home for dinner at least every couple of weeks, while Sybil often didn't make it home for more than Christmas dinner.

She nodded, beginning to tidy up our bowls and glasses. I snatched my wine glass away from her as she scowled in annoyance at me and took a long gulp. The evening was full of surprises, and I wasn't sure if I could handle another one without its haze of liquid courage.

I flopped down on her couch, careful not to spill my wine, and she came back from her kitchen, lowering herself gracefully down next to me. "So, where are you going and how long will you be gone?"

"One month, maybe longer. We'll be in Stockholm for a convention and conferences." She began to spout off a long list of names that sounded impossible to spell or understand. Sybil had always been the smart, studious type, but not in the way that got her bullied throughout the school, as some unfortunate kids faced. No, Sybil didn't do anything by halves. She'd been the local beauty queen, homecoming queen, and head cheerleader all while pulling straight A's and winning science fairs. But something had changed her junior year of high school and she'd dropped the pageant circuit and thrown away her crown. That's when she applied and got accepted with a full ride into Georgia Tech. I'd never forgotten the look of smug satisfaction she had on her face when her acceptance letter came.

Watching her now as she talked about her plans and the fellow scientists she was excited to meet on this trip, I wondered just if I'd ever really understood what went on behind those beautiful eyes. When we were little, we used to play tricks on people. We'd switch places, wearing matching clothes, trying to fool everyone that we met in the typical twinnish antics, even though we weren't technically twins. We did everything together until we'd begun to realize that there were just some things we didn't agree on. Sybil didn't like it when I wanted to do things differently, or when I began to change and get crushes on boys, or have different friends. She'd always say, "But you're MY Hannah. Not theirs. Mine." and I'd have to comfort her, or get her ice cream, or somehow appease her to stop the tears.

Then one day it had all stopped, and she'd become this aloof, other worldly creature I didn't quite understand. At first, I thought that she'd finally come to terms with our differences, but the more distant she became, the more I found myself reaching out to her. It was partly why I'd chosen to work at the FBI office here in Atlanta instead of anywhere else. If Sybil was here, then that's where I wanted to be. Being there for Sybil was the most important thing in the world to me. I couldn't imagine my life without her in it.

CHAPTER THREE

Hannah

"Kelly, my office, now."

David's voice came in low and rough over the phone. I'd been sitting at my desk going over every note I had on the Hildago file, trying to find where in the chain of custody had I possibly misplaced any documents or evidence. But there was nothing I could see. Every item had been logged and accounted for. So I'd begun to look at any of the assisting officers on the case, trying to find a discrepancy or name that hadn't been verified or seemed unfamiliar. At his request, I felt a queasy knot begin to form in my stomach.

I didn't bother knocking but opened the door to his office, slipping inside and sitting down on one of the chairs opposite his desk. He was looking down at a file in front of him with a deep frown creasing his forehead. His dark eyes met mine over the papers and the frown creased even more. The queasy feeling grew.

"Is that the evidence log?" I nodded at the file. When the evidence tampering accusations had started flying the day prior, I'd asked David to pull the logs to see who had been in the locker after I had transferred everything in my possession.

"It is. You're going to want to see this." He reached across his desk to hand it to me and I took it, sitting back in the chair as I began to glance down the list of signatures, names, and timestamps.

My mouth dropped open in shock. There it was in crisp black ink, my serial number, and name. It looked like I had signed in to the evidence room at 11:50 pm on June 11th. Exactly one week after I'd submitted everything in the first place. My eyes found David's again as I held up the pages and shook them.

"Is this some sort of joke? David, this wasn't me! You have to know that!" The sick feeling was quickly turning into outrage and, if I was being honest, fear. The ice queen's accusations had kept me up, even though I knew I shouldn't have worried about anything she said.

David sighed and spread his hands on his desk. "Hannah, I know..." a sudden loud, frantic knock on his door cut his voice off. The frown turned from one of worry to instant annoyance at the unwanted interruption. "If this isn't an emergency, you need to come back. I'm in a meeting."

The door cracked open and the bald head of one of my co-workers peaked around it. "Sir, I'm sorry, but this is an emergency."

"Well, what is it?" David's voice was sharp and impatient.

"It's Agent Kelly." The agent's serious blue gaze turned towards me, and he pushed the door open wider. "It's your sister, Sybil. There's been an accident."

——————

"Sybil! Sybil stop!" I was running, my bare feet met sharp rock as I ran down our gravel driveway to catch my sister who'd just stormed out of the house.

"No, Hannah. You should have listened to me."

"I didn't mean it, Sissy, I didn't! I don't care if you want to punch me or break my toy. But please don't do this!!" She was moving towards a fence on the edge of our property and fear, genuine fear, overwhelmed me. Something wiggled in her arms. "Sissy, please! please! I'll..."

"It's too late. You're MY Hannah, MINE."

"Hannah...."

"Hannah!" The sludge all around me slipped away, and I came back to focus, pulled out of my memory, one I hadn't thought of in years. I blinked, eyes that were dry and gritty like I'd been crying for hours, but my cheeks were dry. David was kneeling in front of me holding out a cup of water and I just stared at it, trying to pull at the edges of memory I'd been in, so I could go back further and remember. What had I been upset about? But it just kept slipping away. I'd felt this feeling, this grief, once before, but I couldn't remember what it was or what had happened.

"Hannah, there's a detective that wants to talk to you." He'd stopped trying to get me to take the cup of water and set it on the curb where I was sitting, looking nothing like the fortress of calm stability he normally projected. When I just stared at him numbly, he continued, "You don't have to talk to her yet, but if there's anything you can tell her now, it might help get them looking for who is responsible faster."

"Okay." My voice sounded small and distant in my ears. I looked over David's shoulder at an African American woman who was approaching us. She was short, with dark brown hair cut in a pixie style and the tips dyed blonde. Other than me and David, she was the only one not in a uniform. I briefly registered that we probably shopped at the same place, because I recognized the navy blue suit with red pinstripes she was wearing as one that I'd had my eye on. It would look fabulous with my red heels. Thinking of the color red caused a sudden sharp and intense pain to lance through my chest. "Sissy, stop! Please!" The sound of my memory bounced off the walls of my mind like an echo.

Sensing my distress, David stood and faced the detective. "I don't think she's able to tell you anything right now."

I had to give the woman credit. She didn't balk at his largeness, but her eyes were kind when she stepped around him and knelt in front of me, taking over David's earlier position.

"Hannah? Special Agent Hannah Kelly?" She used my official title like it might be a lifeline to me, reminding me that we had a connection through the brotherhood of law enforcement even though we were strangers. "I'm Detective Angie Kesler. I'm going to be assigned to your sister's case." She reached into her pocket and pulled out a business card, holding it out to me. "Look, I don't expect you to have answers right now, but if you can tell us anything about your sisters' activities over the past 24 hours, it might help us start piecing together a timeline of events leading up to the break-in."

I took the card and nodded, licking dry lips before croaking out, "What...", the words felt like they were sticking like bile in my throat, "You think it was a break-in?"

Seeming to understand what I was saying, the detective gave a curt nod and stood up, partially indicating the townhome building that was now surrounded by yellow police tape and Atlanta's finest.

"To be honest, Ms. Kelly, that's what it looks like on

the surface. The place is a mess. We won't know more until CSI gets in and does their stuff. And we will need to talk to her neighbors and try to find witnesses. So far, no one heard or saw anything." She paused and turned back around to me. "When was the last time you saw your sister?"

"Last night." A dry sob caught in my throat. "It was ice cream night."

At the description of Sybil's pristine environment, violated by intruders, I felt some numbness begin to slip away, and something far more dark and dangerous replaced it. My nails dug into my skin as I clenched my fists.

"How did...." God bless the detective. She knew what I was asking before I could get it out. "We can't be certain until the coroner does their full examination, but it looks like blunt force trauma to the head. There wasn't much to identify from her facial features." At my sob, she paused as if remembering she wasn't reporting to one of her colleagues, but the grieving sister of a murder victim.

"It looks like she put up a hell of a fight." She offered in a soft voice, like the fact that my beautiful and brilliant sister had fought off her attacker until her last breath might comfort me. I wasn't, and as the window to my world spiraled closed into a foggy haze, that dark thing that was unfurling inside of me whispered, It should have been you. I was too far gone in my grief to realize the voice sounded just like Sybil.

———

I sat in the passenger seat of David's car waiting for him to finish coordinating whatever needed to happen once the crime scene analysis team finished their job. David had taken on the pseudo role of acting on my behalf while I retreated into the numb depths of my shock. I watched as a steady stream of crime scene techs dressed in their white forensic suits carried boxes and bags of evidence from my sister's townhouse to the waiting vehicles.

Just a few short hours ago, I had been walking with her down those steps to my Uber driver, where I'd paused to give her a brief hug.

"You'll call me as soon as you get there, right?"

Sybil rolled her eyes and gave me a light push towards the car. "Yes, I'll call you as soon as I get settled."

Smiling, I opened the door and looked down at my app to verify my driver before sliding into the backseat. I closed the door but rolled the window down, motioning for Sybil to come closer as I leaned my head out and gave her a cheeky grin.

"Okay, and just so you know, I forgive you for skipping out of the country on me, but I won't forgive you if you aren't back by your birthday."

Sybil let out a very unladylike snort and shook her head. "And miss all the fun? Of course not!"

Her birthday was a little over a month away and it was our tradition for me to make a ridiculous deal out of it while she begrudgingly went along with whatever wild idea I had planned. To be honest, I made a big deal out of all birthdays because I felt like they should be celebrated fully. With balloons and streamers and cake. Lots and lots of cake. Sybil was probably going to hate me for what I had planned this year, but once she got over her initial anger, I knew she'd loved the thrill of it. What better way to greet another year older than by jumping out of a perfectly good airplane? Satisfied she'd be back in time to celebrate, I blew her a kiss and rolled the window up as the driver sped off from the curb towards my tiny apartment closer to the city center.

The memory caused my eyes to begin to burn again with unshed tears. David returned and slid into the driver's seat next to me. As he turned the car on and began to head towards the expressway he was talking, and it took a moment to realize I hadn't heard a word he'd said.

"I'm sorry. What was that?"

David's eyes flicked towards me before going back to the road. He cleared his throat, "I said that if you wanted, we could have someone dispatched to your parent's house. Normally, the detective handling the case would notify them, but I told her you may want to do it."

I looked out the window and watched the cars zoom past me. Tell my parents what? Tell them that their princess was gone? Tell them that their oldest daughter, you know- the one with the badge and gun, the one charged with protecting people, had left her there to die at the hands of some thugs? It should have been you.

"No, I'll tell them."

David nodded, more to himself than me, I think.

"What about her boyfriend?" I asked, suddenly breaking a long stretch of silence as the car slowed in the heavy evening traffic.

"Boyfriend?" David flicked on his turn signal and began maneuvering towards an exit ramp, which at this time of day was more dangerous than a high-speed chase. Atlanta drivers in rush hour traffic were cranky.

"Yes, Sybil was supposed to be leaving today to meet him in Europe for a research trip. Simon." I frowned, trying to think of his last name, not sure if Sybil had ever told me more than his first. The only time I had ever even had a glimpse of him was when I'd answered her phone for her one day while she was getting ready to meet him. He'd seemed just as surprised to hear my voice as I'd been to hear his decadent, gravely, and slightly annoyed tone of his. I'd chalked up how much I'd liked the sound of it to his foreignness and had quickly handed the phone over to my sister. But now I had no way of contacting him or even knowing where to start, other than asking some of her other colleagues. And if he was already in Europe, he may be there waiting for her and not known until the news reached him from the university.

"I don't know about a boyfriend, but I did get a call from the office about someone your sister worked with that wanted to speak to you." It was then that I realized that I hadn't been paying attention to where we were headed, just assuming that David was taking me back to my apartment.

"What do you mean? Why would they want to speak to me and not Detective Kesler?"

He shook his head. "I'm not sure. Just that they said it had to be you and it had to be now.." He pulled into his parking space and I was momentarily distracted by the mysterious co-worker.

We entered the building and rode the back elevator to our floor. I was thankful everyone seemed to be gone for the weekend. The last thing I wanted was sympathetic looks or awkward conversations. Walking down the hall, we entered one of our secure interrogation rooms and I arched an eyebrow at David. This was the only room that didn't have cameras or hidden recording devices in it. We used it solely for informants who we had to debrief discretely.

"What's going on here? Why can't I meet them in your office?"

David shrugged. "He said what he needed to tell you had to be done in private. This is the most private room we have. I'll be right back. I was told he's waiting in the reception area."

Moving into the room, I took a seat at the table, my back to the door, and rested my head in my hands. The emotional fatigue of the past few hours was starting to catch up to me, and all I wanted to do was sit somewhere dark and quiet. But I still had to talk to my parents.

Lost in thoughts of how I'd break the news to my mom and dad, I didn't hear the door whisper open or catch the click of it shutting softly behind me.

"Hello, Hannah." My back stiffened as I straightened up in surprise. That voice, I'd only heard it once and only for a few brief moments, but I recognized the dark timber and the slight lilt of a Scottish accent as if I'd listened to it a thousand times a day. The way it curled around my name sent a shiver down my spine and I turned around to stare in shock at the man in the room with me. He was big, maybe as big as David, but lean where David was all bulk. I briefly recognized that he had dark hair, gray eyes, and was possibly one of the most attractive men I'd ever seen. But none of that mattered, because I knew without a doubt who this man was and that he wasn't supposed to be here.

CHAPTER FOUR

Simon

The first thing I noticed when I stepped into the room was her scent. Jasmine, with hints of vanilla, teased my senses, and I inwardly frowned at how appealing I found it. The second thing I noticed was that while yes, based on all surveillance footage and photos I'd gathered, she looked almost exactly like her sister; the differences were so striking that I felt like a fool for thinking they could be mistaken for being the same person at all.

Her hair was long and fell in soft waves past her shoulders. Where Sybil would have never tolerated even a single strand being out of place, Hannah's looked like she often had her long fingers brushing through it in a hurried attempt to make it somewhat presentable. I wondered for a brief moment if it was her perfume I was scenting in the small room or her shampoo.

The eye color was different, too. Sybil had green, almost grey eyes that often reminded me of something cold and reptilian-like. Her flat and emotionless gaze could make even the most hardened criminal flinch. Hannah's, however, were so expressive they almost burned through me, and they weren't a true green. Instead, there were flecks of hazel and gold ringing in her pupil, making them flash. Which they were doing right now, first with shock and now with what looked like fury.

I cleared my throat and moved further into the room while carefully cataloging the details I'd missed in my observations of the other Ms. Kelly. She made it easier by standing with such a force that the chair she was sitting in tipped back and fell over.

"You. Are. Simon." She bit out. Her voice was low and husky, just like I'd heard over the phone a few short weeks ago. If I thought she sounded sexy then, it was off the charts in person. Her hands were pressed flat against the table as she leaned forward and stared at me, one corner of her soft lip curling in a snarl. I flicked the barest of glances at the full swell of her breasts against her white blouse, my eyes catching on the gold necklace resting against her exposed skin with the Saint Michaels pendant flashing before moving back to those captivating and angry eyes. The combination of sex appeal and fury made my head spin. It was the kind of temptation that I couldn't afford and I quickly tamped down on any dark desires before they could rise to the surface.

"Yes, lass, I am." I was cut off by the force of her body slamming into mine, catching me off guard as I was pushed into the wall with enough force to make my head bounce against it. Hooking her foot on the inside of mine, she kicked my leg out and threw me off balance, using the momentum to push against my shoulder and turn me with a hard shove so that now my chest and face were pressed into the wall. What had just bloody happened? I winced as she yanked hard on my arms, pulling them up my back.

"David!" Her voice cracked as she called out to her boss. "David! Get in here!"

I gritted my teeth in slight annoyance, but let her continue. I needed her pliant and willing for the rest of this meeting. What was the expression? Do you get more flies with honey? I'd had every intention of being the sweetness she'd needed to open up. Normally, Evan would have been sent in for a job like this. But since Hannah had already heard my voice over the phone, we'd thought it best that I am the one to talk to her first. However, all thoughts of playing the nice guy were quickly going down the drain. Still, I had to try. "Hannah, you don't want to do this-" She cut me off with a sharp punch to my lower back, straight to my kidneys and I grunted in pain.

"Shut up." Her voice was a snarl of fury and emotion. "I don't know who the fuck you are really, but I can tell you one thing. My sister was murdered and her - boyfriend-" she said the word like it was poison she was trying to spit out "who was supposed to be in fucking Switzerland and waiting on her, is here, looking not the least bit bothered by the fact that the woman he's been dating for weeks is dead."

Her whole body pressed further into mine with every word and dammit if I didn't feel every single inch of those soft curves I'd gotten a glimpse of earlier pressed against me.

"And you know what that makes you, in my opinion? A fucking suspect or a really shitty boyfriend. Probably both."

The word boyfriend made me frown because it was the furthest thing from the truth. I was here to try to gather intel from Hannah and determine how much information Sybil passed on to her. But it seemed like either Hannah was a brilliant actress, or Sybil had been lying to her sister as well.

Sybil Kelly had been as cold and calculated as they came and until I could sort through what was truth and what was a lie, I had to assume Hannah was the same. Letting her think I was Sybil's lover may play to my advantage, because with Sybil now gone, I would need every single point I could get. But when I felt the cold metal of handcuffs begin to slip onto my wrist, I realized it was time to let the nice guy act go.

I pushed hard against the wall in one sudden movement, my size and strength to the advantage. She was strong, for sure, but I was stronger. As soon as I had space, I whirled and grabbed her arm, yanking her forward and spinning her fast until her front was slammed against the wall, just as I had been. Her gasp of shock made my lips twitch slightly. I took advantage of the situation by pressing firmly against her, just as she had done to me, sliding one of my legs between hers, secretly enjoying the way her body stiffened up as I nudged them apart. Her whole body vibrated with her fury and for the first time in a very long time, I found myself smiling. Before she could scream or call for her partner again, I yanked her arm a little higher on her back and slapped my palm over her mouth.

"Tell me, lass, do you always judge first and ask questions later?" I growled and lowered my head until my mouth was just against her ear. Purposefully, I drew in a deep breath of that delicious jasmine and vanilla scent. I could feel her heart speeding up and noticed a flush of goosebumps appear across her skin as awareness of how I was pressed against her came over her. Her eyes, though, were still shooting daggers at me, so I didn't stop or give her space. She reminded me of a cornered tiger and I wondered if I wasn't making a mistake by trying to catch her by her tail. "And you've got it wrong. I was never in Stockholm waiting for her. Sybil was supposed to go with me. She never showed up for the flight." It was partially true. We were supposed to meet at the convention. I just hadn't left for it yet. The fact that Sybil had told her sister about the convention set off several alarms. I needed to find out what else Sybil had told Hannah. "I'm here because there's information about your sister you need to know. And there are questions I need to ask you about her. Starting with, what do you know about the Abromov group?"

I could tell that curiosity over my statement and question was warring with the initial rage and suspicion she'd felt, so I eased up slightly and dropped my hand from her mouth.

"There's nothing I don't know about my sister and stop calling me lass. Who the hell says that, anyway? Is that like a pickup line or something for you? Does it get you laid?" Her eyes were defiant, daring me to challenge her. "And who the fuck is the Abromov group?"

I let her go, but not before pressing into her once more. It was hard to resist. Something about her fire and defiance called to me. Not to mention she was drop-dead gorgeous. I hadn't had a reaction to a woman like this in, well, ever honestly. The instinct to want to press her buttons more just to see how she'd react rode me hard. But instead, I stepped back to give her as much space as the small room would allow.

Slowly, she turned around and kept her back pressed against the wall. Her eyes blazing with fury.

Aye, not a lass. More like a hellion.

CHAPTER FIVE

Hannah

I turned around and kept my back pressed against the wall even though he'd given me space. It didn't seem like enough, and I wished my body could sink through the plaster and wood to get to the interrogation room on the other side. Maybe it was my heightened state of emotions, but his presence was overwhelming. I'd barely gotten more than a glimpse of him before I'd launched myself at him in an attempt to detain him until David could get back into the room. But as he'd turned the tables and switched our positions, I was very aware of each pressure point where his solid frame had pressed into mine.

My body still tingled from the feel of his thigh sliding between my legs. His lips barely brushing the tip of my ear had sent literal chills down my spine, and not in the 'I should be terrified that I'm in a locked room with my sister's potential killer' way, either. And the way my body had reacted to him pressing his hips into mine was unsettling on so many levels. Which made me wonder if I was going crazy because there was no doubt about it. He was dangerous. Not to mention my dead sister's boyfriend. Ew, Hannah, just ew.

I watched as Simon slowly unzipped the black leather jacket he was wearing, noting appreciatively the dark t-shirt that was molded to a broad chest and pulled out a thick file folder from somewhere within before motioning to the table. Who the fuck wears leather in the middle of summer in Georgia? Now that the haze of anger was fading, I was catching details I hadn't noticed before.

"No ascot."

He paused from picking up the chair I'd tipped over and dark eyebrows arched over steel-colored irises. "Pardon?"

My eyes traced from the collar of his leather jacket, down to the dark denim jeans that hugged his muscular thighs. The memory of the way that thigh had felt pressed between my legs made my heart race again, and I swallowed harshly before meeting his gaze once more. By the way, his lips quirked and his eyes gleamed, I was sure he could tell exactly what I was thinking, but I tried to ignore it and waved a hand in his general direction.

"The way Sybil described you, I had always pictured you in some fancy suit and ascot, with a cane and top hat or something." I was gifted with a brief smile, more grimace really, as he began to pull out some papers and what looked like photographs from the folder, laying them carefully down on the table.

"Yes, well, when the occasion calls for it." Lord, help me his voice. The man could make a killing as one of those romance novel book narrators. I had to immediately shut that train of thought down. I would not think of my dead sister's boyfriend saying "Good girl". Just no, not happening. I needed to get back in control of this situation and fast.

"I want David in here before we discuss anything else. I'd also like to see some identification."

He glanced up, smirking, his gaze unreadable as he pulled out the chair for me. "I'm sorry lass, but David isn't going to be able to sit in on this conversation with you, and you won't find any identification on me, I'm afraid."

"Why the fuck not?" I'd taken one step away from the wall towards the door, eyeing it to see if I could make it past him fast enough to get out of the room. No matter how charming or sexy he was, I knew in my gut this man had something to do with Sybil's death. If he wasn't directly responsible, then he somehow knew who was. The coincidences and timing were too suspicious. I just need to get out of here and find David. There was no way he could have known who this man was when he allowed him in here for this meeting. Hell, I'd barely known who he was.

"Language, please." He chastised, and I nearly choked in surprise. Was I just told to watch my swearing? "Because what I'm about to tell you, lass, is on a need-to-know basis. And David doesn't need to know. Trust me, he's already taken it up with my employer." The smirk widened to a sinister grin, and I could feel the red haze of rage creeping up again. Fuck this guy and his games.

"I'm not your lass, and just who the hell is your boss?"

He shrugged and waved me towards the chair once more. "Sometimes I'm my own boss, sometimes I'm not. In this instance, the organization I work for is currently having a conversation with Special Agent Williams on the scope and function of his role from here on out, as well as yours. Now please, sit. I'm sure you would like to finish this chat before you have to make the call to your parents, lass."

I was sure that he added that last "lass" as a dig at me, but at the mention of my parents, the desire to fight seemed to leave my body, and I felt the weight of grief settle around me once more. Subdued, I moved towards the chair he held out for me and sat down.

He moved around and sat opposite of me, all amusement and arrogance gone from his expression. "Now, what do you know about the Abromov group?"

"Fuck you. Answer my questions first. Why weren't you in Stockholm like Sybil said?" Did I continue to cuss in retaliation for calling me lass again? Maybe.

He didn't flinch at the question but pushed a black-and-white photo towards me.

"Language. You may think you're in charge here, lass," he drew the word out like a sharp dagger, "but I assure you- you are not." The dark, underlying threat in his tone was there. "Do you know who this is?"

I wanted to retort that I was the Federal Agent, and this was my interrogation room, but seeing a group of men and women in white lab coats standing on the steps of a concrete building distracted me. One or two were smiling. Most had the pinched academic expression of people who only wanted to get back to whatever their research project was. In the middle of the group was a grey-haired man in a dark business suit, a stark contrast to all the white surrounding him. The building behind them was plain-looking but had writing in a foreign language that looked like it might be Russian in tall block letters across the front. I frowned, unsure of what I was looking at. It reminded me of a cold war era photo but I could tell by the clothes and general appearance of the people it was more modern times.

"I have no clue," I said honestly, confused by what he

was showing me. Another picture was slid on top of that one. It was the same group of people, only they were standing in front of what looked like the Georgia Tech Research Institute building. It was a building I was very familiar with as my sister had her office there, and we'd occasionally meet for lunch outside of it. Instinctively, I looked for her among the group of researchers, trying to find a connection between what Simon was showing me and her. But she wasn't there.

"This is the Abromov Group. They are scientists and researchers with a wide range of specialties ranging from genetics, biochemistry, and nuclear science, to geospatial engineering, from all around the world. They are headed by that man there." He tapped a finger on the face of the grey-haired man. "Sergei Abromov is a Russian philanthropist who assembled the team based on researching and creating new technologies for the betterment of mankind. They are responsible for many of the world's advances in medicine, science, engineering and even combating climate change."

I sat back and narrowed my eyes at him, still not seeing the point of what he was saying and how that had anything at all to do with Sybil.

"Okay, so they're a bunch of smart people doing cool shit for humanity. You still haven't told me how this ties to my sister or anything about why you weren't in Stockholm like you were supposed to be."

His eyes darted to my lips and did I see a hint of desire flicker through their grey depths? No, it couldn't be. He just didn't like hearing a woman cuss. It wasn't ladylike. I inwardly snorted. If he thought he was getting a southern belle debutant like my sister, boy was Mr. Posh Pants in a for a surprise.

"Your sister was a member of the Abromov group. And I told you. I wasn't supposed to be in Stockholm yet." He stated simply.

"Are you calling my sister a liar? And am I supposed to know what that means? What the hell is the Abromov group?" Inwardly, I was filtering through all the information I knew about Sybil's job. I couldn't remember her ever mentioning anything resembling the Abromov group or a Sergei.

He opened the file folder once more and took out a few more photos as well as documents and slid them towards me. The photographs showed Sybil dressed in a white lab coat and standing next to Sergei Abromov. My gut clenched as I looked at her. She was so beautiful, with her hair pulled in a soft twist and her hand tucked intimately into the crook of his elbow. But even as I choked back a wave of grief, another thought crept up. Why had Sybil never told me about this?

My thoughts were racing as I stared at the picture of my sister and this Russian man. If Sybil had never mentioned this, what else hadn't she told me? Could she have lied about when she was meeting Simon? No, there was no way. He was the liar here.

I shook my head and pushed the papers back towards him, not wanting to see anything more, not daring to let my mind wander where it wanted to go. "You need to start explaining this shit right now. Pictures of my sister with old scientists aren't exactly life-altering information."

Simon leaned forward and folded his hands in front of him. His eyes were hard and unforgiving. "What do you know about your sister's work and who she worked with?"

"I think the better question is what do -you- know, Simon? You were a part of her team at Georgia Tech, correct? You were supposed to be in Stockholm with her. Why don't you start answering some questions instead of asking them?" I leaned forward and matched his posture, my hands folded exactly like his, so close that they were almost touching each other on the small table. "Because I can sure as shit tell you that with everything you've shown me, you aren't telling me half of what you know or think."

He stared me down for a minute and I swear it was the longest minute of my life. It felt like his eyes were boring straight into my soul, assessing every little dark and dirty detail, bagging it, tagging it, and processing it into whatever neat little filing system of information he had in his head. So long as he stayed out of my panty drawer I was fine with it. Let him think what he wanted. Although at the thought of Simon anywhere near my panties, I felt my cheeks heat. *Again, ew Hannah, just ew.*

"Fine. You're right, there is more to it than Sybil just being a part of this research group." He leaned back and crossed his arms. "As you may have deduced," I snickered, and his eyes flashed in mild annoyance at the interruption. "Something funny?"

I sat back and mimicked him, "Well, you may not wear an ascot, but maybe a bowler cap and pipe would suit you better. You sounded like Sherlock Holmes, 'deduced'." I air quoted as I said the word and then waved at him to continue.

He glowered at me, but began again. "As you may have *realized*, the Abromov Group isn't just a philanthropic pet project for Sergei Abromov. It is a cover for both corporate and government espionage. They recruited the brightest and most impressionable minds to their cause and then lured them into stealing government technological secrets under the guise of research, or sometimes outright bribery and blackmail. That's how Sybil was introduced. She was identified early on by the group as someone who they could exploit."

At this, I sat straight up and slammed my hand onto the table. "Wait, are you saying my sister was a spy and

stealing government secrets to sell to foreign governments? Are you saying she was a traitor?"

He shook his head and sat forward again, grey eyes
glinting in the fluorescent light. "Nay, lass, you have it
wrong. Your sister was in the Abromov group, yes, but
she was also a source for the CIA. She was spying on the
Abromov Group for them. Her job was to determine
what new technologies the Abromov group was
exploiting and selling to other governments.

CHAPTER SIX

Hannah

The entire drive to my parents' place, I'd stewed over the revelation that Simon had given me. My sister was a spy. Well, technically not a spy, but an asset. A source. One with ties to terrorist groups and enemy governments all over the world. And with the information Simon was sharing, I could only assume he'd been her handler, although he wasn't coming right out and saying it. Maybe because of their relationship? I wasn't sure. But I'd stared at him in shocked silence. How the hell had I missed this?

Simon then launched into a string of rapid-fire questions with such intensity that it left me feeling even more battered and bruised after an already long and emotionally draining day. Who did my sister talk to? Who were her friends? Did she have any other known associates outside of her work? What and how much did I know about her work at the college? At the last one, I had had enough and stood up, shoving the papers towards him.

"Look, Simon, I literally found out my sister was murdered and living a double life for the past five years, all in just over an hour. I'm not answering any of your questions until A. you answer some of mine or B. I get the fuck out of this place so I can go tell my parents their daughter is dead. But unless one of those things happens, we're done here."

After a few heartbeats of silence, where once again I was given his intense and almost intrusive stare, he nodded and collected the files back into their folder. "Fine, I'm sorry. I shouldn't have pressed you, but you'll understand if I'm interested in knowing more about Sybil outside of work." He didn't look at me, but the air was heavy with his meaning. As her boyfriend. Maybe I'd misjudged him and the intensity of his questioning was more because he was trying to make sense of what had happened to my sister as well.

"Yeah, well, apparently I'm not the one to ask. Because of all of this?" I waved my hand at the table and its contents. "Is a complete and total mind fuck to me right now."

He had looked like he was going to comment on my language again as he stood and moved to stand just a few inches in front of me, but instead, his eyes darted down to my lips and then back up to meet my gaze once more. "How is it, lass, that you and your sister could look so alike, and yet be so utterly different?"

I tipped my head back to look up at him, suddenly sure I'd met the only other man outside of David who had ever made me feel tiny in his presence. Self-consciously, I licked my lips and his eyes seemed to follow the movement.

"Well, Momma always said Sybil got all the sweet because I took all the spice. And stop calling me lass. Seriously, you need better pickup lines. Go read a romance novel or something. Ask a Reddit forum. 'How to not sound like an 18th-century douche-bag and get laid.'" I almost winced as the words flew out of my mouth. I didn't know what it was about this man that set me so on edge, but my natural reaction was to put as much verbal distance between us as possible. I also wasn't overly concerned with hurting his feelings because he really was a douche-bag. A very sexy douche-bag, though.

"Hmm... would you like to recommend a book or two? You look like the type who might chug one out in the middle of the night when you're all alone and have scared off any bloke who wants to star in your fantasy." He cocked a lazy eyebrow up and gave me a mocking grin. "Let me guess, you're the Dark Highland Warrior type? Or no, I have it! It's the Rakish Duke?" Before I could respond one of his fingers came under my chin to tip it up further and that same tingly awareness from when he had been pressed against me earlier came back with a vengeance. "It's a shame too. I promise the real thing is better. Maybe one day I'll show you how much better."

Before the shock his statement could register he'd moved away and opened the door.

"I know we've gone over this, but you understand that what I've told you is completely confidential. You are not to speak to anyone outside of myself about this matter unless my organization has fully cleared them. We have given you information on a need-to-know basis only because of your unique position as a federal agent and your relationship as her sister. Any further information will be given to you at such a time as is deemed necessary."

"I know what the fuck need-to-know means, asshat," I muttered under my breath as I moved past him, wanting to get out of that room and away from him, away from the sexual tension that was thick in the air, and away from that damned file of my sisters' secret life as quickly as possible.

"Good, lass, then we shall be in touch." He followed me into the hallway and it was all I could do to keep from flipping him the middle finger as I stalked down the hall towards the exit and my car. But I didn't do it, if only for my sister's sake. Something about this man set me on edge and while I could see how Sissy or any woman would be attracted to him physically, because yeah, he was hot as fuck. But what she could have possibly seen in his personality was beyond me. Not to mention the fact that she could date a guy who could so obviously hit on her sister when she wasn't even six feet under was a little disturbing. Maybe it was purely physical in the attraction and nothing more. Had I read into Sybil's relationship more than what was there?

When I'd finally arrived at my parents' home in a quiet rural community about an hour and a half outside of Atlanta, all thoughts of Sybil and her secret life had taken a back seat to the all-consuming pang of loss and grief. My parents reacted as I'd expected them to. My mom had collapsed on the floor and my father had stalked off in a quiet rage before coming back to envelop us both in his arms. We'd cried together until there were no more tears left in our bodies and our voices were hoarse with unanswered questions. In the end, I'd told them I would stay for the weekend and help them begin making arrangements for her funeral.

I was sitting on their front porch swing, looking out over the large green lawn hedged in by dogwoods, the next morning when my phone rang. The morning air was already thick with humidity, which was typical of a Georgia summer, but I wanted to take in the view a few minutes longer before escaping into the cool of the house.

"Hey, David."

"Hey, kid. Got a minute?" I cracked a rueful smile. In the office and around our co-workers David was 100% the professional. On the weekends and after work, though, he relaxed into the easy friendship we'd come to know over the past couple of years.

"Yea, I got a minute."

"How are you doing?" I knew David would be worried about me, but I also knew it wasn't like him to call when a text would do.

"I'm as okay as I'm going to be, David. Tell Marie I said thanks for checking on me." My smile turned genuine as I heard a woman's voice in the background.

"We're here for you Hannah, you know you have a home here anytime you need us. We're family, baby girl." Marie was David's wife and had decided as soon as she'd met me that my country bumpkin self had needed someone to look out for me. Atlanta was too big for a small-town girl like me. No matter how many times I told her I wasn't alone, that I had Sybil here too, she'd just scoff and roll her eyes. "Your sister is in her own world, girly. Yeah, she's family, but you need others who have your back, you know? It's different." And as much as it hurt my heart at the moment to admit it, I did need them.

"Thanks, Marie, I know you are. Are we still on for dinner this week?" After a few minutes of chatting and filling her in on the tentative funeral plans, she handed David back the phone.

He paused for a moment and cleared his throat, probably waiting until there was some privacy for what he wanted to say.

"Spit it out, David. It's hotter than Satan's tits out here and I don't want to go back into the house and risk waking up my parents." It had been a long night and as I'd laid in my bed in my old bedroom, now a guest room, I'd heard their voices murmuring and crying softly until the early hours of the morning.

David just cleared his throat again and let out a big sigh. "Listen, Hannah, I'm just going to say it. I know this is a bad time, but this is coming down from higher than me..."

I cut him off quickly, "Did that fucker Simon say something to you? Because I'm telling you right now, David, he's suspect number one in my book. I don't care who he works for or what level of clearance he has. Something is off about him."

"What? No, no... you've got it wrong. I don't know much about him other than someone from the D.C. office vouched for him." His sour tone told me just how disgruntled he was over that. "You were told anything at all out of courtesy, not that I know what you were told, just that it needed to stay between you and Mr. Gallagher." He huffed, and I had the mental image that he was pacing on the small patch of rug in their living room. Whatever David had to tell me, it was making him very uncomfortable and nervous, so I just waited for him to continue.

"Hannah, we pulled the CCTV footage from the evidence locker." At this, I stood and inwardly relaxed. He was talking about the misunderstanding in the evidence room. In all the craziness of the past 24 hours, I'd forgotten about it. Was that all? Good, then they'd see that there's no way I'd been the one to sign out the Hildago evidence. "Ok great, did they see who signed my name?"

"Hannah, the only one on the camera footage for that day is you."

For the second time in twenty-four hours, I was left speechless. It took David calling my name several times before I responded.

"Are you fucking kidding me? David, that's impossible. You know I would never jeopardize this case like that!" With each statement, I could feel panic begin to overwhelm me and my voice rose higher and higher until I was practically shrieking.

"I know kid, I know. Listen, just calm down, okay? I'm going to get to the bottom of this, but until then, and with your sister's murder, maybe it's a good idea for you to take some time off. Let things calm down a bit and spend some time with your parents."

"Oh come on David, don't bullshit me. I'm being put on suspension, aren't I?" Honestly, I couldn't blame him. If I had been David, it's exactly what I'd do in his position. No matter what I believed, the evidence was stacked pretty strongly against me, and considering how high profile the investigation was, someone was putting pressure on our department pretty hard to find a scapegoat. And it looked like the easiest one to single out was me.

"Technically, it's a leave of absence. Considering the circumstances of your sister's death, I managed to get them to agree with that." He seemed to hesitate a bit before continuing. "Your sister's boyfriend may have pulled some strings as well."

I collapsed back into the front porch swing in shock. "He did what? Why would he do that? No, actually, who the fuck is this guy David?"

"I don't know Hannah, I don't." I could practically see David's frown through the phone. He didn't like being in the dark any more than I did. "But whoever he is and whatever your sister's connection to him was, I don't think you should get involved."

"Why would I get involved? Sybil's life was her own. She didn't want me involved, anyway. Or she would have told me something, or at least given me a hint about what she was doing." I had to stop before I went into too much detail. Simon had made it very clear in his debriefing because that's what I realized it was now, not just a boyfriend sharing information with a grieving sister, that I was the only one to know the level of involvement Sybil had in the Abromov Group. I pressed my lips together in a thin line of distaste. I didn't like keeping things from David, but I knew he'd respect the rules enough not to press. Not unless it was necessary.

Once again, the conversation paused and until David sighed. "Hannah, listen, I've got to go. But whatever was with Simon and Sybil, maybe it's just better that's where it stays. Sometimes we go digging into the wrong secrets and we end up digging our own graves. I'm going to do my best to get to the bottom of this evidence room fiasco. Give your mom and dad my condolences and let Marie know about the arrangements."

He hung up, and I shivered in the late morning humidity. What would happen if I went digging into Sybil's secret life? Would I finally uncover that thing that I had always sensed hiding behind her eyes? What about her murder? The break-in theory seemed to be too clean and neat, especially knowing now what she was involved in. And then there was Simon. Who was he? Why didn't he seem as broken up about it as someone at least close to Sybil should be? Why was I secretly just a bit ok with that?

"One day I'll have to be the judge of that."

My fists tightened until I could feel my nails biting into my palms. Everything in me said that Simon and this Abromov Group business had something to do with Sybil's death. I just needed a way to figure out how to prove it. And unfortunately, that meant that I'd need to get back to Atlanta as soon as possible and track down Simon. I had more questions than I did answers at this point, and the only one who held them was a cocky devil with a mouth made for sin.

CHAPTER SEVEN

Hannah

It turned out tracking down Simon Gallagher wasn't as difficult as I thought it would be. I'd left my parent's house Sunday afternoon, promising to meet up with them when it was time to collect Sybil's belongings. Because of the nature of the case, it would be some time before Atlanta PD would be done analyzing everything, and we'd decided to hold off on the full wake and funeral for now. Knowing Sybil, she'd probably planned to donate her body to science or have it cremated anyway, but there was nothing we could do until we were told the coroner had released it.

I frowned, holding the white piece of cardstock that had been tucked into my doorjamb with just S. Gallagher and a phone number embossed on it. The plan I'd come up with over the weekend had seemed so simple, but now

I was wondering if it was too simple. According to some
research I'd done on the Abromov Group, they never
met in public except once every three to five years, and
that was mostly to receive some awards or recognition
for their contributions to science. The only one ever in
the public eye for the group consistently was Sergei
Abromov himself. Most of the scientists and researchers
who took part did so from the comfort of their own labs
and universities all across the globe.

The next scheduled meeting for the group was at an
awards banquet and charity event in Stockholm, Sweden.
Several of the group members were going to be presented
with awards for their work in the field of genetics and
the advancement of vaccine research in relation to the
global pandemic. This was presumably where Sissy had
been headed and now I was determined to go in her
place. It was the only way I could think of to get close to
Simon and find out more about what my sister was
involved with.

But now that I was standing here about to make the
phone call to schedule our meeting and somehow
convince Simon that I could get him the information he
needed, I thought maybe I was in over my head. I wasn't
an undercover agent, nor had I ever worked any undercover assignments. Who was I to assume that he even
needed any help? He never specified what my sister actually did, other than relay information on the groups'

activities to him. Despite the newness of their relationship, the way Simon had talked about Sybil, it was as if he knew her more intimately than I'd realized. And that would make sense if they'd been in communication for some time before he arrived here. There must be something they were planning or working on that would cause Sybil to travel with him to Europe. It was the only thing that made sense and not the relationship that Sybil had led me to believe she was in.

I didn't have to time to contemplate my plan further though when a knock on the door sounded. Tossing the card down onto my coffee table, I checked my door camera and gasped in shock. Looked like my decision was made for me, or he was just too impatient to wait for my phone call because standing outside my door was the man himself.

I swung the door open sharply just as he was about to knock again and glared at him. Despite wanting to contact him and put my crazy plan into action, I wasn't looking forward to interacting with him again. But the way his dark eyes lit up told me he didn't feel the same. "So glad to see you're home, lass."

"What do you want, Mr. Gallagher?" I was determined not to let "lass" get to me this time.

"Aren't you going to invite me in?"

I nearly snorted and gave him a quick once over, appreciating that he didn't have on a jacket today to cover up the plain t-shirt that stretched over broad shoulders and a thick chest. "I'm not sure, Mr. Gallagher. Are you a vampire?"

If my question surprised him, he didn't show it. But he flashed pearly teeth as he grinned and answered devilishly, "Are we a Vampire Diaries' fan, lass? I can assure you, I don't bite unless you want me to." The last part was probably meant as a joke, but the way he leaned towards me as he said it had my stomach doing somersaults and my forgotten libido came roaring back to life. *Jesus, I needed to get laid. Get a grip, Hannah.* I didn't even realize he was brushing past me until I turned to watch him stroll into my living room as if he owned the space.

"Stop calling me lass. And I wouldn't want you to bite me even if you were a hot vampire."

He walked to my bookcase and picked up a picture of my sister and me, but he turned around and cocked one eyebrow up in amusement. "Ah well, thank you for the compliment, lass. But you may want to tone down the flirting if we're going to have a professional relationship. Can't have rumors of impropriety getting back to your bosses now, right? Wouldn't want to feed that little black widow rumor."

I gaped at him, horrified. I hadn't even realized what I said or how it sounded. The man's presence and personality were so infuriating I couldn't think straight and every time he called me a lass, all I could feel was borderline rage building under my skin. And what did he mean by professional relationship? Who the fuck did he think he was? I opened my mouth to say exactly that before remembering that a professional relationship was what I wanted. But I couldn't let him know that yet. I needed to feel this out first.

"What the fuck to do you mean, professional relationship, and you know damn well I wasn't flirting!" I snarled, happy to have an outlet for my frustration and embarrassment.

I crossed over to the bookcase and pulled the picture frame from his hands, placing it back on the shelf, but immediately regretted it because he'd moved on to thumbing through some of my books. The particular one he'd picked up was a dark fantasy romance that more or less was fictional smut with heart. Normally I wouldn't have cared what people thought about my reading choices, but seeing him skimming through the pages felt way more intimate than it should have.

"Would you like to borrow it? Like I said before, I'm sure you could learn a thing or two." The conversation we'd had about my choice in reading material made my anger flare brighter and I glared at him, willing him to put it down. Instead, he turned another page and glanced up over the edge of the book at me, that dark glint in his eyes once more.

"Oh no, lass. No need for me to borrow it, I much

prefer the real thing. You might try it sometime." He glanced down at the pages, slipping my bookmark to the place where he'd flipped to before snapping it shut. "Is this where you get the vampire fantasy?" Sliding the book back onto the shelf, he turned towards my couch and sat down, looking entirely too comfortable in my space. I glared at him and began to pace around my living room, picking up discarded items and clutter.

"Sure, just invite yourself in and make yourself at home. Read my books, touch my things, threaten my reputation, and accuse me of flirting. I was not flirting." When I was extremely stressed or flustered, I tended to mutter to myself and stress clean. Simon watched me with an amused expression for several minutes before clearing his throat and catching my attention.

"You asked about a professional relationship?" One brow arched at me, waiting for me to remember the reason he was here.

I swept a few takeout containers from my kitchen counter into the trash bin and turned to look at him. "Yes, please explain that, because as far as I'm concerned, the last thing I want is the word 'relationship' attached to you in any manner whatsoever."

He chuckled and leaned forward, bracing both elbows on his knees before his face morphed into a deadly serious mask. "You may call it whatever you like, lass. I'm here to offer you a proposition, one that would see you working for me and my organization. We need you to pick up where your sister left off."

I snorted, but my heart beat just a little faster. Could he really be here offering me what I was going to propose to him? I fingered the Saint Michael's pendant around my neck in a silent prayer of thanks for the good luck.

"Mr. Gallagher, your 007 Bond game sounds fabulous, but I already have a job. One I'm very good at. I'm not interested in working for you or any other organization. Not to mention, I'm not a scientist."

"That's not what I hear, black widow. And it's not the science we need you for, it's your body."

"Excuse me? Exactly what do you mean?" I tried to sound indignant and not rise to his bait as I finished tidying the counters off, hoping that my face wasn't betraying any of my thoughts or emotions.

"You've been put on an indefinite leave of absence, lass." He leaned back, looking way too casual and good on my sofa. I refused to acknowledge that, however, and went back to pick up a stack of bills I'd yet to organize as he continued, "And there's no denying you could be a carbon copy of your sister. Your help would be invaluable in finishing the work we've started."

"That was a mistake. As soon as they find the discrepancy in the evidence log, I'll be back to work. And if you think I could walk into Georgia Tech and just pick up where my sister left off, then you are delusional or a terrible spy. Probably both."

"First, you won't be going to Georgia Tech. You'll be traveling to Sweden. And what happens when they find out there wasn't a discrepancy, or that someone did not fudge those logs and camera recordings? What then?" I hated how confident he sounded and as much as I wanted to just come out and say yes, I still couldn't seem too eager and the desire to defend myself was strong.

"I didn't do that and just as soon as I find out who the fuck is behind this, I'm putting them and the Hildago Syndicate away for good."

"What if I told you I could help you do that? What if I told you I could help you uncover your mole? Would you be more inclined to my proposition then?" He looked like a cat that had caught the canary. The smug smirk that lifted from the corner of his lips made dimples flash in his cheeks. He knew, even if I hadn't already wanted to say yes, that this little carrot he dangled would be the incentive I'd need to consider what he was saying.

I sat down in an overstuffed armchair next to the couch and frowned, thinking over the possibility. Could he help me unmask who was trying to sabotage me? He certainly seemed like he would have the resources. The chances were just as high that he was saying anything he could to get me to agree. Empty gifts and promises were the trademarks of someone in his profession when they were cultivating a new source. Still, the idea of killing two birds with one stone was way too tempting of an idea to pass up. Prove Simon was involved in my sister's death and find the person sabotaging my career? It was a done deal.

I rubbed my sweaty palms on the fabric of my jeans and took a few calming breaths before looking back at him, where he was watching me with an unreadable expression. "You really think you can find out who is framing me?"

He nodded slowly, his gaze never changing, and somehow I knew he was telling me the truth.

"And you honestly think I could help finish Sybil's work for you?"

Again, that slow nod.

"Fine, then I accept, on one condition, though."

He cocked his head slightly in what I could only assume was amused curiosity. "Oh? And what is that, lass?"

"You stop fucking calling me lass."

CHAPTER EIGHT

Simon

Whatever thoughts I had managed to convince myself over the weekend about my attraction to Hannah Kelly had dissolved the minute she'd opened the door and speared me with the intensity of her gaze. I drank in her presence like a man dying of thirst, delighted to see that instead of a suit, she was wearing a thin black tank top tucked into jeans that hugged every curve of her delicious body. The woman had sunk her claws somewhere deep into the dark part of me that bordered on obsession, and if she knew what was good for her, she would slam the door in my face and forget any conversation we'd ever had about her sister.

Instead, she'd matched me word for word, aggression

for aggression. And if the way her eyes kept drifting over me, like she was cataloging everything she saw much the same way I did to her, then the interest wasn't just one-sided. I almost lied and made up another reason to be here, when she told me didn't have a desire for any type of relationship, professional or otherwise, with me. Whether or not she realized it, that was probably the wisest decision she could have made.

Initially, my plans were to investigate Hannah Kelly. Then to get close to her and pressure her for information that her sister may have passed on. I had been convinced they had a close and trusting relationship. But then I quickly realized Sybil was as closed off in her personal life as she was in her secret one. There was no way Hannah knew just how involved her sister was in the corrupt organization. In the interrogation room, it had been very apparent that Hannah had been in the dark about her sisters' work. Her genuine shock and confusion caused me to rethink my approach, and I'd needed to think fast to twist the narrative. Sure, she could be deceiving me, even now, but my gut told me that wasn't the case.

When I'd found out that the federal case she'd been working on had come to a standstill because of some evidence tampering, I'd called a friend of mine high in the D.C. office of the FBI to get her a leave of absence rather than a full suspension. I didn't doubt that she was innocent and the victim of some high-pressure political manipulation. But that was the bureau for you. It was all black and white until enough money changed hands and then it wasn't. I would have been content to leave her to her own devices and face the agency's wrath, where they'd probably shove her down to some filing room in a backwater field office if she had given me any sign of being anything like Sybil in any way but her appearance.

Because there was no doubt about it. Sybil was a dangerous and murderous woman. The years of undercover work I'd done attempting to get close to the Abromov group, trying to find out who was behind some of the world's most deadly chemical and biological weapons getting into the hands of terrorists, had finally led me to a breakthrough. And I was now one step closer to my revenge. Sergei Abromov may have been the face of the operation, but Dr. Sybil Kelly was the beautiful, twisted mind.

But here I was with a near carbon copy of Sybil and the years of deep undercover maneuvering and plans wouldn't be for anything after all. All I had to do was convince Hannah that she was the key to completing Sybil's fake mission and maybe play on her natural American patriotism. Westerners were so easy to manipulate that way. I frowned and found myself staring at the deceased woman's sister while she moved around the small apartment cleaning up half discarded takeout containers, trying to unravel the puzzle. Something just didn't make sense. Everything I knew about Sybil Kelly was in direct contradiction to the sexy hellion in front of me.

When she'd finally sat down and began to seriously consider my proposal, I felt a moment of guilt. Hannah would not understand the level of depravity that her sister had stooped to, and I would do my very best to make sure she never did. Right now, though, I needed Hannah's cooperation, because I knew that the spider's web that Sybil had created was still active and crawling with dark and dangerous deals. I needed Hannah to replace her sister to get the evidence to shut down the Abromov Group for good.

And it could work too. The similarities between the two women were uncanny. I would have called their mother a liar if I hadn't seen the birth certificates and records myself. Whatever genetics the Kelly family had, both daughters were abundantly blessed with them. I was once again momentarily distracted by those blessings and the way her thin tank top dipped low, revealing the tops of full breasts that made my mouth water. The gold chain with her Saint Michaels pendant rested between the valley between them and I briefly imagined her wearing nothing but that necklace. *Get it together Gallagher*. I shifted to hide the sudden hardness pressing against the fly of my jeans and hoped the way my thoughts had wandered wasn't showing on my face. The sooner

Hannah Kelly got the information I needed, the sooner I could disappear and not get distracted by dangerous entanglements.

But then she opened her sexy little mouth and told me to stop "fucking" calling her lass as part of her agreement and I knew the darkness in me would not want to let her go.

Rising from the couch, I moved to where she perched on the edge of her chair, delighting in the way her breath hitched as I crowded her space, intentionally standing too close. I couldn't help it. Every time her smart mouth challenged me, all I wanted to do was push her more. To find her breaking point and watch as she fell apart. Then carefully, so carefully, put her back together. I was a sick fuck, and I knew it.

"I accept your condition, princess." The darkness crept into my smile as I leaned down, taking a lock of her hair and watching as it slid like silk between my fingertips.

The look she gave me could have peeled skin from bones.

"I didn't say you could call me princess either. It's just Hannah, or Agent Kelly if you prefer. But nothing else." Never anything else was left unspoken between us.

"Then you need to learn to negotiate better, princess." To her credit, she didn't let my taunting get to her much. Something held her back from saying what she truly wanted to. Instead, she sat back in her chair like a queen in her castle and gave me a haughty look.

"Ok, partner... so how does this work? I'm just suddenly read on to some super-secret squirrel mission? What's the process?" I arched a brow at the new name she gave me, clearly trying to play me at my own game.

"You'll be fully debriefed in the morning. For now, all you need to know is that you'll be picking up where Sybil left off, leaving for Sweden and the ICHSST conference. The actual conference doesn't occur until later this month. However, before that, there are lectures, dinners, and formal events to attend." She nodded her head and leaned forward, elbows braced on her knees, and the look on her face was all business. "Yes, I've done my own research already. The Abromov Group hasn't met in over five years. Possibly longer with the pandemic. This will be the first conference any of them have attended in a long time and presumably together, other than Sergei."

She ran long fingers through her hair and frowned. "I'm assuming that since Sybil didn't join the group until sometime in 2016, she hasn't met any of them other than Sergei in person. This means that none of them will actually recognize her, or they will just be confused by the time between meetings. I mean, we look enough alike that unless someone knew her intimately, I should be able to pass." I couldn't deny being impressed. Hannah had done her research and had quickly deduced why I'd wanted to utilize her.

"But," I could hear the skepticism in her voice as she stood and began to pace the small space in front of her couch. "I don't understand what you expect me to do. I'm not Sybil. I don't know fuck all about her work, or academic journals, or any of the shit these people are going to expect me to know. The minute they ask me more than a few surface questions, they're going to figure out that I'm a fake."

"Well, if you continue to use that kind of foul language, princess, then they most certainly will." I drawled out and crossed my arms. Did I care she swore? Not really. But it bothered her that she thought I cared and seeing her skin flush with anger was becoming a guilty pleasure of mine. I wondered if she flushed the same way when she was screaming her release.

"You'll be fully debriefed, beginning tomorrow and brought up to speed before it's time to go. My team will see to it." I made my way to the front door. It was time to update everyone and get them filled in on the change in plans. They'd be pissed about the risks, but wouldn't want to see this operation fail. We'd all been singularly focused on this one mission for too long. "Be ready at 0400 sharp. I dislike to be kept waiting."

I left to a string of curses and "-sadistic fuck, who does a mission brief at 4 am?"

CHAPTER NINE

Hannah

I watched him speed off on a blacked-out Triumph motorcycle from my window and finally understood the need for leather and jeans in the middle of summer in Georgia. I wanted to be annoyed that he had the typical sexy secret agent toys, but somehow it only made him hotter. And dammit, hot was not what I needed to be thinking about him right now. What I needed was to get as much information about him as possible before tomorrow morning.

I briefly wondered if this was how he'd gotten to Sybil. Had he bullied, charmed, and wholly up-ended her world the way he was doing to me? Or had he pulled the mysterious, brooding, intellectual act and gotten her to fall for his brains over his brawn? A pang of grief gripped me as I remembered what she'd said to me about my choice of romantic partners. It seemed I would not be learning my lesson any time soon. I wasn't sure who I was more annoyed with, myself for the ridiculous attraction I felt towards him, or Simon for the complete lack of regard he seemed to have for my sister's memory.

I picked up my phone and shot a quick text to David, letting him know what I needed and asking him to check in on my parents for me. Then I sent another text to my mother telling her I might be busy for the next few days with work. They didn't know they had given me a leave of absence, so it was easy to get away with explaining things as work-related. Maybe I was being overly cautious, but something told me I needed to be prepared for anything to come the next morning and I didn't want them to worry if I didn't respond for a few days.

After finishing the cleaning I'd started while Simon had been here, I sat down on my couch with a glass of wine and attempted to get lost in a show on Netflix while I waited for David to reply. Hopefully, whatever contacts he had in other units could come through with the information. In the past two meetings I'd had with Simon, he'd been the one to hold all the cards. I wanted to be the one in the know for once.

The T.V. droned on and eventually, the sun sank. I felt my eyes drift close.

"Hannah!" Sybil's voice called out to me in a sing-song way. "Where are you, Hannah? I have a surprise for you!"

I was sitting under one of the tall pine trees in our backyard. A stick next to me where I had been absentmindedly digging in the ground. My tears had dried on my face, leaving streaks of dirt in their path. I didn't look up as the shiny bright shoes approached me and came to a stop. I didn't say a word even when she huffed in annoyance and knelt in front of me, so careful to not let her sundress get close to the red Georgia clay.

"Come on Hannah, I have a surprise for you!" Finally, I raised my eyes to meet hers. She was smiling and holding out something in a brown paper bag. I eyed it warily. I didn't trust her, not after what she'd done earlier. I tossed a glance past her towards the neighbors' fence and felt a fresh wave of tears begin to form.

"I don't want it, Sybil. Just go away."

She shook the bag and pushed it into my face. "Trust me, Hannah, you're going to want this."

"What is it?" I continued to eye the bag warily but reached out anyway to take it from her. Her smile grew wide, her teeth perfectly straight and shining white. Was she trying to make up for what she'd done? Was this her attempt at an apology?

"Let's just call it a promise. You'll see."

My gut churned with confusion and angst. I didn't want to take the bag, but she was practically shoving it in my hands. Something told me to just drop it, that I didn't want to see what was inside. But she looked so sincere. I eyed her warily, looking for any deceit or malice in her delicate features, but she just continue to smile encouragingly at me. Sniffing, I wiped my nose and pulled the bag to me, offering her half a smile in return, a little curious, and mildly hopeful, at what she could have gotten me. Carefully, in the bright Georgia sun, I opened the crinkled top of the bag, slowly looking inside its shadowy depths. And then I screamed.

I woke with a start, my throat feeling raw and sore, like I'd been screaming for hours. Sweat covered me even in the cool air-conditioned apartment and I could hear my heart pounding in my ears. The nightmare had felt so real, so lifelike. Sybil's smile burned into my brain like a brand. Another noise pulled me out of the shaky dream-scape, and I realized my phone was buzzing on the table next to the couch.

Running a shaking hand through my hair, I swore a silent prayer of thanks to Saint Michael at the text notif-ication. David had gotten back to me.

David: Simon Gallagher isn't who he says he is.

Me: I fucking knew it!

David: You don't know half of it. He's a ghost.

Me: What? Are you sure?

David: Positive. My source said they only call him in when they can't have anything tied back to them.

Me: Do you have anything on him at all? I need something, David, anything.

David: All I have is hearsay and rumors. There's nothing concrete, no files. You know how they do these things.

And I did know. A ghost was someone who was untraceable. They technically didn't exist anywhere. All their records and files were wiped completely clean, and it stayed that way. Governments used them when they couldn't afford to get their hands dirty. His comment about his boss made sense now. He didn't have one.

Me: I'll take whatever you've got. My sister was dating this ass-hole for christ's sake.

David: You can't use this as evidence. If you think he's connected to her death, you're going to need something concrete. And Hannah, if he is a ghost- you might not want to start looking. Some things need to just stay buried.

I knew what David was saying. Whatever secrets Sybil had taken with her to her grave might be for the best. I could just tell Simon that I was out, that he'd need to finish his mission without Sybil and without me. But what if it was already too late? What if he'd told me enough information to make me expendable? Would he kill me if I was no longer useful to him? Or would he kill me no matter what? I felt like I was back in my dream again. Sybil's face hovering over mine as she held out the mysterious paper bag. I didn't want to open up her secrets, only to be horrified by what I found, but it might already be too late.

Me: All things done in the dark come to the light

eventually, but sometimes you have to get a little dirty to expose it. She was my sister David; I need to know.

David's response came a few minutes later.

David: Fine. But don't say I didn't warn you.

David: Simon Gallagher (if that's even his name) is former British Special Forces. SRR to be exact. Then he did a stint in MI6. After that, things get a little muddier. There's a rumor of him being under investigation for war crimes and conspiracy to commit treason. Something about his team getting involved in gunrunning and then conspiring to let a terrorist escape. They say he killed the team member who ratted on him.

Me: Oh, is that all? He sounds like a choirboy.

David: Not funny Hannah. If even half of those rumors are true, he's still a very dangerous man.

Me: I take it none of these charges stuck though? Doesn't seem like something the British government would let slide.

David: No. Nothing stuck. Either they didn't have enough evidence or he had enough leverage to weasel his way out of it. He's been working as a mercenary since. Whoever hires him either does so because of his past, or they choose to overlook it because of his effectiveness. He gets his mark, every time.

Me: Got it. He's slippery, possibly a murderer, definitely a psycho.

David: Definitely a murderer. He kills people for a living. You need to be careful, Hannah.

Me: Always. Thnx D.

My mind was racing. The past 72hrs had been information overload. First Sybil's death. Then finding out that she was a part of some undercover spy ring. Now discovering that her boyfriend and partner were some sort of war criminal turned mercenary. Because that was what a ghost was. They existed outside of government organizations because most of the time what they did wasn't sanctioned anywhere. They were hitmen, assassins.

I rose from my spot on the couch and paced, trying to lie out the timeline of events as best I knew them, but at this point, I still had too many unanswered questions and loose ends. I only knew two things. One, Simon Gallagher, was now even more firmly placed in the suspect category of my sister's potential killer. And two, my sister's life hadn't been as neat and tidy as she'd been leading everyone to believe.

I walked over to the picture Simon had been looking at earlier and picked it up, my eyes going right to Sybil. Her arms were crossed, and she was standing stiffly beside me. I didn't seem to notice though because my arm was thrown around her waist and I was smiling from ear to ear. It had been her graduation day from high school and we were standing in our parent's yard, by the large pine tree. Behind us, in the distance, I could see the neighbor's fence; though I'd never noticed it before, there was a large black shape hidden in the shadow of its slats. My hands began to shake, and I quickly put the picture down as I was filled with a deep sense of dread.

Something was lurking in my mind, like the shadow behind that fence. Something that I couldn't help but feel was tied deeper to Sybil, me, and now this Abromov group business. Glancing at the clock, I knew it was late, but I also knew that I wasn't going to be able to just lay down and sleep. Grabbing my laptop from its spot on the counter, I flopped down on my couch and flipped it open. Armed with what little information I knew, I decided to do some digging of my own. I was an FBI Agent, after all, it was time to start acting like it.

CHAPTER TEN

Hannah

That morning I woke up at 3 am sharp after passing out on my couch. I couldn't remember the exact details of what I dreamed about, just that they hadn't been pleasant. Every dark corner of my mind saw either my sister's taunting face with a brown paper bag, a large shape hovering in the darkness, or Simon's gray eyes watching me with burning intensity. Stalking me. It had all blurred together until the blare of my alarm clock had finally pierced the fog of sleep.

I yawned, exhausted, and begrudgingly began to get ready for Simon to show up. Early mornings weren't out of the norm for me by anyway means, but more often than not I was a night owl on a stakeout somewhere. Criminals loved to stick to the classic cliches; for the most part, the same could be said for cops and FBI agents.

After showering and pouring a cup of coffee, I checked my phone and noticed a text from my dad, asking me to call him when I got a chance. Glancing at the clock and realizing I still had a few minutes before Simon would arrive, I hit the send button and let it ring. My dad had always been an early riser, a habit left over from his years in the military. He'd probably been up before I had.

"Morning sweet pea." I smiled. I knew my dad was taking Sybil's death hard, and it was good to hear his voice without the tears this morning.

"Hey, Daddy. I got your message. What's up?"

"I just," he cleared his throat, "Hannah, listen, I'm going to come right out and say it. I know you're going to want to know who was responsible for your sister's death and believe me, I do too, but I don't want you doing anything crazy."

I frowned. What was he talking about? Did Dad know something about Sybil's secret life? Had she confided in him? "Dad, what are you talking about? I want justice, don't you?"

"Baby, that's not what I mean. Of course, I want justice, and we'll get it. I just don't want you putting your career at risk chasing down Sybil's shadow. You did that enough growing up and now that Sybil's," he paused, the emotions starting to get to him, "... gone, maybe you can finally come out of it."

I frowned, not understanding what has sparked this conversation with my dad. "Dad, I don't understand. Sybil was my baby sister. If anything, she grew up under my shadow. That's how it works." I tried to laugh around the grief and pain his words were causing me. How could anyone say that I just needed to let this go? First, it had been David. Now it was my father.

"Hannah, you were so enamored with Sybil that you didn't see it. But your mother and I did. Anything Sybil wanted, you gave her. Your ice-cream? It was hers. Your favorite toys? Hers. When Sybil went away for her competitions, you were like a lost puppy, moping around until she came home. Hell, Hannah, you even moved to Atlanta because of her. You could have gone anywhere, anywhere! But you chose to move where Sybil was."

I sputtered, shocked and confused. She was my baby sister. I was supposed to take care of her, protect her, and love her. And that's what I'd done. Right?

"Dad, I didn't move to Atlanta just for Sybil. You guys were close by too! And I like Atlanta. It's home now."

"Sweet pea, I know you. You never liked Atlanta. You always talked about moving to the beach or going somewhere different. San Francisco or maybe San Diego. But the minute you found out Sybil was accepted into

Georgia Tech, it's like that was it for you. All your plans suddenly involved moving to Atlanta to be near her."

I didn't know what to say. This was the first time I'd ever heard my father say anything about my choices or life decisions. He'd been encouraging and supportive when I'd said I wanted a career in law enforcement. It had even been his suggestion that I apply for the FBI. But my relationship with Sybil, or my reasons for moving, were never discussed.

"Dad, I... yes, my initial plans were never to move to Atlanta, or even stay in Georgia. But, I'm ok with it. This is just how life had worked out. And honestly, Dad, if giving up the beach meant I got to spend even five more minutes with my sister here and alive, I'd give it up for the rest of my life. I'd trade it all for her."

My dad sighed wearily, the weight of whatever was eating at him evident through the phone. "That's just it Hannah. You shouldn't have to trade it all to have a relationship with someone. Not even someone who is your blood. Ask yourself this before you go risking and trading away anything more for her. Would Sybil have done it for you? There are plenty of colleges with amazing research programs. Would she have followed you?"

Before I could respond, a sharp knock sounded at the door and I realized what time it was. "Shit, Dad I'm sorry. I've got to go. Listen, I don't know how long I'll be busy with work, but we will talk about this more when I can get away. Ok? And don't plan the memorial or wake without me. I'll call you as soon as I can."

"Ok, Hannah. I love you. I love Sybil. Just think about what I said before you do anything rash."

The knock sounded again, louder and more insistent this time. "Ok Dad, I promise, I have to go. I love you too."

I hung up and opened the door to a stony-faced Simon glaring daggers at me. Once again, I was struck by his gorgeousness. His dark hair was slicked back and shiny, like he'd just combed it from the shower. He was freshly shaven, and I didn't realize how much I liked that. I always thought I was more of a beard girl, but the sight of his clean-cut jawline made me want to brush my lips against it just to see if it was as smooth and silky as I imagined. My eyes traced down from his jaw to his lips, firm, and turned down in a slight frown of disapproval. Shit, that's right, he didn't like to be kept waiting.

"Sorry, I was just on the phone with my Dad." I moved aside so he could come in, but instead of doing so he gave me one long glance from the top of my head to the bottom of my feet and his frown deepened.

"Go change into something more appropriate and pull your hair up. Be downstairs ready to go in 3 minutes." He then shoved something into my hands, pivoting on the heel of his boot and headed back to the elevator at the end of the hall. I was left standing in bewilderment, wondering what the hell was wrong with what I was wearing, until I looked down and realized what he'd handed me. It was a motorcycle helmet. *Oh, hell no.*

I stepped out into the hallway and called down to him just as the elevator reached my floor. "I am not riding on a motorcycle with you. That is out of the question! Just give me the address of where we're going and I'll meet you there." The doors glided open, and he didn't turn around, just reached inside and pushed the button for the bottom floor. "Two minutes, princess." Then the doors shut, and he was gone.

CHAPTER ELEVEN

Hannah

"Fucking mother fucking fucker." I got really creative with my swearing when I was pissed and flustered. Racing back into the apartment, I was striping out of my clothes as fast as I could undo the buttons of my blouse and pull down the zipper to my skirt. My heels were kicked off, and I shoved my legs into the closest thing I could find, which happened to be a pair of ripped jeans. Not exactly the professional look I was going for, but at this point, I didn't care. I was not letting him get away or giving up my only chance to find out who killed Sybil. Yanking one arm through a band t-shirt that had been draped over a laundry basket, I prayed to whatever laundry god there was that it was at least clean and didn't have profanity on it. Next came socks, and I was never more thankful for my obsession with shoes than now because I had a pair of Converse in just about every color waiting to go. I grabbed the first pair I could find, the helmet I'd dropped on the ground, and raced out the door to the elevator.

By the time I'd reached the bottom level of my apartment building, I was sure I looked like a sorority girl doing the walk of shame. Or pride. It depended on perspective; I guess. My socks were mismatched, and my shoes were only half tied and leopard print. I realized too late I'd forgotten to pull my hair up. Oh well. I didn't relish the thought of tangled biker hair, but I had little choice. And if he didn't like my appearance then, well, he could just deal with it. It's not like he'd told me what kind of transportation we'd be taking.

When I burst through the lobby doors of my building, I found him waiting outside with his bike running, long legs straddling the seat, and his helmet already on. He had the visor down so that I couldn't see his expression, but somehow I still felt the disapproving burn of his stare. He revved the engine as I pulled down my helmet, tucking my hair the best I could, and swung my leg over behind him. Then he was taking off before my ass barely touched the seat and I lurched forward to catch my balance, my hands instinctively reaching around to grab his waist for something to hang on to.

I inwardly seethed at the sudden contact. He was purposely being an ass. And for what? Because I was a few minutes late and didn't know biker chic attire was a part of the dress code? I wanted desperately to slam my fist into his back in a repeat of our first encounter together, but didn't want to risk an accident. Although something told me he was more than capable of taking a punch to the kidneys while maneuvering at high rates of speed on a two-wheeled death machine.

Instead, I concentrated on not falling off. Which was difficult to do when I was simultaneously forced to slide closer to his hard back, my legs braced against muscular outer thighs and my hands with nowhere to go but around his waist. Everywhere we connected seemed to burn, just like when he'd had me pinned against the wall. I tried to adjust and pull away from the close contact, both not wanting to touch him as much as possible, but also wanting to touch him as much as possible. I ended up with my whole body perched stiff and upright, muscles clenched tight as I clung to the back of the bike, praying that the next turn wouldn't be the one where I was ejected.

"You need to relax."

His growling voice startled me and I flinched, nearly throwing myself despite my best efforts not to. Great, there's a mic. I wondered how much of my cussing he'd heard while I was trying not to fly off the back.

"Lean into me, but keep your weight centered. Try to feel the shift of the bike. When I move, move with me." I grimaced, not wanting to touch him any more than I had to, but realizing that he was right. If I didn't relax and lean into him, I was going to end up wrecking us both, and my jeans had enough rips in them as it was.

Carefully I leaned forward and shifted my hips back, my center of gravity instantly going lower, my chest was now pressed to his upper back. I still didn't want to hold on to his waist but knew I needed to put my hands somewhere, so opted for the top of his thighs. Now I could feel his muscles bunch and relax as the bike shifted, and I began to instinctively move with him. It wasn't ideal, but it was more comfortable and I did begin to feel myself relax.

"Thanks," I told him through the mic. He merely grunted and began to weave in and out of the early morning traffic that was beginning to build on the expressway. I had a moment of realization of how absurd the situation was. Here I was on the back of a bike with a mysterious secret agent, speeding off on a dangerous mission to apprehend an international criminal. It was like something straight out of a spy movie. I couldn't help but snicker at the thought.

"Something funny?" The annoyance in his voice from earlier was gone, replaced by mild curiosity.

"Am I a Bond girl?"

"A what?"

"You know, a Bond girl. 007? Secret Agent? Golden Finger?"

I heard a barking laugh come from the mic and something low in my core clenched in response. So Mr. Posh Pants found something other than intimidating me funny. I decided I liked the sound of his laughter.

"I promise you, princess, I'm no James Bond."

"No?" I couldn't keep the smile out of my voice. "What are you then?"

"I'm better, although I've been told I do have golden fingers."

I scoffed at his arrogance as he made a sharp turn off an exit ramp, forcing me to grip him a little tighter. I liked the way his muscles felt under my hands and it took every ounce of self-control I had not to let them wander higher, to the hard ridges of his abs and up to the thick planes of his chest. His little comments about having golden fingers sent my brain into overdrive, imagining exactly how good he would be. *Get a hold of yourself, Hannah. You are not allowed to be attracted to the sexy assassin for hire. Remember Sybil!*

"Better than James Bond? I doubt it. Tell me one thing you do that's better than Britain's greatest spy."

"Easy. I never get involved with women."

"What? How does that make you better?"

"It's his one weakness. He gets involved with every damsel or villainess in distress and then gets caught in the crossfire. Relationships are dangerous. So I don't have them."

"But you were involved with my sister." I frowned. Surely that counted as a relationship, right? Or had he really felt nothing for her?

"That was different." He growled and slowed to a stop in front of a hole-in-the-wall Korean restaurant in one of the shittiest neighborhoods I'd ever seen. "We're here." Effectively ending our conversation as he turned off the motorcycle and removed his helmet. I did the same and took a deep breath as I stared at the un-lit storefront. He might not have thought I was a Bond girl, but I couldn't help but feel a small thrill of excitement. I was about to become a spy. *I am so a Bond girl.*

CHAPTER TWELVE

Simon

The minute I'd taken one look at her in that black pencil skirt, red silk blouse, and sexy as fuck heels, I'd known I was done for. I wanted to shove her back into her apartment, smear the red lipstick across her lips and ruin her perfectly put-together look. I wanted to see her come apart beneath me as I ripped the skirt from her body, find her delicious center, and shove my tongue so far inside her she'd forget her own name. She'd forget every name but mine.

The way her green eyes had widened as she drank in my appearance told me her thoughts weren't too far off from mine. Although I doubted they were as graphic, or detailed, as I was imagining. Frustration at my reaction to her and the fact that there was nothing I could do about it surged through me. As I told her to change and stalked off, it was all I could do to not punch a hole through the back of the elevator. I was going to lose my mind.

It had only gotten worse. I thought telling her to change would alleviate the raging hard-on I had from the moment she'd opened the door but no, instead the hellion had to come down in ripped jeans that hugged her curves, a band t-shirt that hung off one sexy shoulder and showed the black strap of her bra underneath. A bra that was quite visible through the graphics of the white shirt. Somehow, she managed to look wild and sexy all at the same time. The way she was rushing towards me, eyes blazing with anger and determination, I was positive she didn't realize it though.

Then I'd had to spend the next fifteen minutes with her pressed against me, shifting, rubbing her body against my back as she tried to maintain her distance. I was a fucking idiot for bringing the bike. I should have picked her up in the car. Or hell, just let her follow me on her own. When she'd finally settled down and relaxed into me as I maneuvered through the city, I kept secretly wishing she'd let her hands creep higher to feel exactly the effect she was having on me. Would it scare her? Or would it lead to giving us both what we clearly wanted? I had a brief fantasy of taking her on the back of the bike and nearly wrecked us right then.

My team was right. There was no way this was going to work. Only their reasons differed completely from mine. After I'd left her apartment the night before, I'd immediately gone back to our safe house to go over the plan and come up with new contingencies. None of them were thrilled with the change or the fact that we'd be working so closely with an inexperienced, first-time undercover agent. Not to mention the lie that they would have to keep up about my actual relationship with Sybil. Not that it would be that big of a deal. They were used to keeping up a ruse. However, the fact that as her sister, Hannah would have some keener insight into Sybil's personal life would make the lie harder to sell. Not to mention the attraction I wasn't going to be able to hide. It hadn't taken me very long to realize that this woman was perfect for me in every way. Every way that could get us both killed.

And I'd almost fucked it up already. When she'd asked me about being a Bond girl I'd been her moaning around my cock deep into my bike fantasy. I was not in my right mind, and that was a mistake I couldn't afford to make with a woman as intelligent and observant as Hannah. I couldn't forget that she was a federal agent and even though she wasn't adept in espionage, she was still highly trained in interrogation techniques and cultivating sources. The sobering thought had been the ice water I'd needed on my dangerous train of thought, and I was thankful that we were now parked in front of one of our safe houses.

I would have preferred to have introduced her to the team at our penthouse in a much nicer part of town. This area screamed seedy back alley drug deals and gangs, but it was the one concession I'd needed to agree to before they were on board. They didn't trust that Hannah wasn't in league with her sister or that she hadn't been the one to help Sybil pass information to her counterparts. Someone had to be helping her, and we still had no better suspect than Hannah. I knew better, though. Every instinct I had told me that Hannah was innocent, but until I had someone else to pin it on, my team wasn't convinced.

I heard a very unladylike snort come from next to me and turned to observe her attempting to detangle her long hair from the wind, whipping it on the ride over.

"Something funny?" I arched a brow as she tugged a hand free and waved it towards the dilapidated building in front of us.

"Yeah, this is fucking hilarious. You expect me to believe a highly classified espionage team is holed up in this shit hole?" She shook her head and crossed her arms under her breasts while giving a look that said she was waiting for me to confess I'd tricked her.

"Yes, that's exactly what I expect you to believe. You're

telling me all your stakeouts were in pristine conditions?" I was moving towards a door next to the entrance to the closed-down restaurant. Pressing my hand against a brick, I didn't bother to look back over my shoulder but could feel her intense gaze watching my every move. The brick pushed in and slid to the side, a small but deceptive camouflage for the biometric keypad that was hidden behind it. It wasn't a safe house we typically liked to use, but it was still as secure as we could make it. My thumbprint was scanned, prompting the door next to me to unlock and swing open, revealing a darkened hallway. I stood to the side and swept my arm before me. "After you, princess."

I couldn't help but smirk when her eyes narrowed at my new nickname for her and she swept past me. I followed close behind; the door swinging shut firmly behind us, plunging the small space into total darkness. Her gasp of surprise sent a thrill straight to my center, bringing back the raging desire from just a few moments ago. I didn't know why getting under her skin appealed to me so much, but once I started it was like I couldn't stop. I was an addict, and it seemed my drug of choice was going to be Hannah Kelly.

"What the fuck, Simon. Where are the lights?" I could hear her fumbling around, attempting to locate a wall or switch in the pitch black, and then before I could respond, she turned and stumbled hard into my chest. I let out a soft grunt as instinctively I wrapped my hands around her arms to keep her from falling.

"Careful princess, it's not safe to go fumbling around in the dark."

The darkness hid her expression, but I could feel her pressed against my chest, her heartbeat drumming loud and fast against mine. For a brief moment, I was lost in a haze of jasmine and vanilla, and I found myself lowering my head toward the intoxicating scent. Her warm, sweet breath fluttered against my cheek and my heightened senses could hear the wet slide of her tongue against her lips as she licked them nervously.

She could have pushed me away. She could have cussed and told me to get the fuck away from her. She could have done any number of things to tell me she didn't want me holding her right now. But instead, she just stayed perfectly still, coiled, tense, and waiting to see what I would do. I turned my head towards the sound of her lips, feeling her suck in a breath as she sensed just how close my mouth was to hers.

"Your heart is being fast."

"Because I'm locked in the dark with a psychopath, obviously."

"Is that it? Or is it because your dirty little mind is thinking about all the fun we could have in the dark?" Her gasp told me all I needed to know. The bike ride over here had been just as much torture for her as it was for me. My hands slid slowly down her arms and I pushed her against the wall that I knew was just behind her back. She didn't resist, her breath coming in short little huffs as she fought against her own desires.

"You're insane. I have no idea what you're talking about." But her voice shook and didn't have the same bite to it as before.

"Really? You don't think I felt the way you held on to me on the bike? If I were to check, how wet would you be right now, princess?" I growled against the curve of her neck and heard a soft moan escape her lips.

Bright lights flooded the hall and, like a tigress, she sprang away with a hiss and snarl on her lips. Her green eyes blazed with fury, but her cheeks were flushed for a different reason.

"What the ever-loving fuck, Si, we've been waiting for ages. What the fuck game are you playing here?" At the sound of Evan's voice, I immediately slammed my mask of cold carelessness into place and turned to look up at one of my team members where he stood at the top of a set of stairs just a little further inside the hall we were standing in.

"No games, just couldn't remember where the light switch was." I straightened my jacket and began to head up the steps to the room above.

"They're right where they've always been, mate, right on the left side of the door," Evan grumbled and turned around, calling out to the rest of the team that we were finally here.

I could hear Hannah's angry stomps behind me and her husky voice growl low, "Yeah Si, just what fucking game are you playing?"

"The same one you are, princess. I'm just ok acknowledging it, are you?" Before she could answer, we were inside the safe house room and my team was standing in a semi-circle in front of us, none of them looking too pleased with me or her. Fuck, I'd almost forgotten about the infrared cameras in the hallway. They would have seen everything that had happened.

CHAPTER THIRTEEN

Hannah

Everything in me wanted to murder Simon Gallagher and dance around his burning body. The man was internally combusting levels of infuriation. If looks could kill, I was positive the one I was giving the back of his dark head would have exploded it several times over now. I felt like I was going insane. How the fuck did Sybil deal with him? The longer I was with him, the more I was convinced that my sister was either using him, or he was using her. I was willing to bet a year's salary it was the latter. There was no way she would have put up with his arrogant, alpha-hole, man-handling.

No, Simon the posh, snobby, aristocratic scientist that Sybil had sold to me didn't reside anywhere in the body of the man before me. I wasn't sure if she had outright lied to me or not. But one thing was certain, the relationship they had was non-existent, and I just needed to somehow get him to admit it. But not now, because right now I was standing in front of three people who looked like they could steal candy from a baby without blinking and did it on the daily.

As my gaze swept over the three members of Simon's team, I tried to size up who would be most likely to be a somewhat friendly ally. I felt a small twinge of hope as I settled on the short, dusky-skinned woman standing between two giants. Her hair was a shocking shade of electric blue and pulled up into twin pigtails that trailed down to her mid-back. I wasn't sure what I was more startled by, her hair color being so brilliantly blue or the fact that she had somehow managed to add little pops of the same color throughout her rather military-esque outfit. Even her black Docker combat boots had the color woven through the laces and stitching. I had a compliment on the tip of my tongue, but then noticed that the look she was giving me could have frozen me in place. Ok, not going to bond over shoe shopping with that one. Next?

I turned to observe the two men standing on either side of her. Jesus, they were large. What kind of diet did secret agents eat that made them so damn tall? The one to blue hair chic's right looked like he stepped right out of a mafia film. He was dark all over, from his olive complexion to his jet black hair. Eyes so dark I couldn't tell where the pupil ended, and the iris began just stared at me with a burning intensity that gave me the impression he was mentally calculating how many ways he could kill me before I even made it to the door. A cold shiver traveled down my spine and I couldn't help but imagine that I was having a staring contest with the grim reaper himself. I quickly blinked and turned toward the remaining team member.

Where Mr. Tall Dark and Murdery was giving me the make peace with your maker vibes, this one was at least smiling. Only as I took in the knife, he was casually spinning in his palm like it was a child's fidget spinner. I realized his smile didn't quite reach the icy blue of his eyes. In fact, I don't think I'd ever seen a gaze so empty or devoid of emotion as the one I was looking at right now. And I'd sat across from some really sick psychopaths in my time in law enforcement.

However, he was still the only one of the trio with anything resembling friendly on his face, so I decided to take my chances with Mr. Serial Killer and offered a hopeful smile in return. He didn't blink or stop fidgeting with his blade, just arched a perfect blonde brow and smiled a little wider. I'm not entirely sure it was meant to be disarming, because at the flash of perfect white teeth, all I got was the sense that I was staring at the toothy grin of a predator who knew he had his prey right where he wanted them. I swallowed hard and resisted the urge to step behind Simon, not that I thought he would do anything to protect me from these psychopaths. More than likely, he was thrilled at the idea of throwing me to the literal wolves.

"Evan, Rue, Mike, this is Special Agent Hannah Kelly." Simon's deep voice washed over me and I wondered if he used my title to remind them of who I was, or me. That's right, I'm Special Agent Hannah Kelly, you fucktards. I might not be a super-secret spy or assassin, but I've got my own skills and you're about to find out I don't intimidate so easily. I straightened my spine and tilted my chin up before leveling them all with an all business stare and nodded to each of them.

"Nice to meet you. I'm looking forward to continuing the work my sister left unfinished."

Rue was the first to break the stare down and just nodded with half a grunt before turning and walking towards a set of monitors arrayed on a table behind them. The entire room was fairly sparse, featuring a couch against one brick exposed wall, and a circular table in the center with a few mismatched chairs around it. On the opposite wall was a doorway that looked like it led into a small kitchen and next to that, another shut door that I could only presume was a bathroom.

We were clearly in a studio apartment they'd converted for their uses. There was only one window that was so covered by years of grime that it didn't need to be blacked out. On the wall opposite the ratty couch was a large corkboard with a map and several papers and pictures pinned to it. On closer inspection, I saw that one of them was mine. They'd caught me outside of Sybil's townhome the night of her murder as I was saying goodbye. I swallowed hard, noting the happy way I was smiling and leaning toward her. Sybil had that pinched look on her face, like I'd just said something that annoyed her. My teasing admonishment about her not missing her birthday came back to me and I felt a twinge of grief, a sharp knife-like pain that cut right through my heart.

"Were you always watching her like this? Even though she was one of your assets?" I turned to look back at Simon and he just gave me a blank, emotionless stare. Oh good, we're back to asshole secret agent. I could handle that. What I couldn't handle was the asshole secret agent holding me in the dark and letting me know he knew exactly how attracted to him I was. When he'd whispered those dirty words, it had taken every ounce of self-control I'd had not to grind against the hardness I'd felt pressed against me. Yeah, so I'd been turned on the entire bike ride over. Didn't mean the prick had to announce it to the world. Evan answered instead of Simon and I turned towards the tall blonde man as he pulled out a chair at the table, indicating for me to sit. A psychopath and a gentleman, nice.

"All of our assets are carefully monitored. In our line of work, we can't be too careful about who we are working with and any hidden agendas they might have. Or develop." He had a smooth British accent, and I was slightly surprised, although I guess I shouldn't have been. He sounded more like the posh foreign scientist than Simon did. I took the chair and tried not to notice as Simon took the one next to me, scooting it a little too close for comfort. I tried to inch mine away but would have just hit the leg of the table and so was stuck with his calf, barely brushing against mine. I turned to glare at him. "Have you ever heard of personal space?"

He merely arched a brow and gave me half a smirk. "You weren't complaining earlier." I huffed, my face on fire, and turned back to Evan, trying to not let him bother me anymore.

"Then if you were watching her so closely, do you have any info on who murdered her?"

Evan gave an apologetic shake of his head and took a seat across from me. "Unfortunately no. After you left that evening we were called away for another," he hesitated with a glance to Simon, ".. mission. We were just as surprised as you when we found out about the attack."

I turned to Simon and raised one brow in question. "What sort of mission meant that you had to stop your surveillance of a high-value asset and leave her exposed like that?" I couldn't help the anger that bled through my voice. If these guys had been monitoring Sybil like they were supposed to do, then she might not be dead right now. My sister might still be alive.

"It's classified." He continued to give me his deadpan stare, not offering a hint of anything more in his answer.

I scoffed, fully pissed now, and turned back to Evan. "Seriously, you guys expect me to believe that bullshit?" Mr. Serial Killer just shrugged and gave me that same emotionless smile he first greeted me with. "As Si said, it's classified. But I can tell you that we did not pick up any chatter or disturbances that would have indicated that she was under a threat or there was a reason for us to increase our over-watch on your sister."

"Meaning what? That her attack wasn't anticipated? Or that you just didn't see it coming." I let the meaning behind my words hang in the air, that you failed. I didn't want to hear the little voice that whispered, but you failed me first.

"I assure you, princess, if there was a planned hit on your sister, we would have known about it." Simon's voice took on a cold, hard edge and for a moment, I thought I saw through the mask to the anger that was bubbling just underneath. What was he angrier about? That Sybil had been murdered? Or that he hadn't been able to anticipate it?

"Right, because you guys are some MI6/CIA super spies." I rolled my eyes and was about to launch into another string of questions when Rue plopped down in front of me with a metal box, a laptop, and a palm scanner.

"Those dumb fucks wish they were us." Her voice was silky smooth with a soft Cajun accent and held a whole lot of disdain. "And you're about to become one now, too little FBI baby. Think you can handle it? Or maybe you should check your handbook." The way her lip curled upwards told me she had more against federal agents, and thereby me, than she did against government spy agencies. The handbook she referred to was the Federal Agent's guide and lifeline. It was literally how we were defined in all aspects of operating as a Federal Agent and it was as dear to a Special Agent as the badge that we carried, probably more so.

I wasn't going to rise to her bait, though. Hostility towards federal agents wasn't something new. If it wasn't other agencies pissed we were involved in their cases, it was the criminals convinced we were just out to set them up. I wondered which category Rue fell into. Shrugging, I met her angry gaze with a calm one.

"I'm here to find my sister's killer and finish her work. So yeah, I can handle it."

She gave me a wicked smile and slid the palm scanner towards me. "Good, because it's time to say goodbye to Federal Agent Hannah Kelly. She doesn't exist anymore."

CHAPTER FOURTEEN

Hannah

"Excuse me?" I visibly balked at the piece of equipment in front of me and then looked at Simon. "What do you mean, I won't exist anymore?"

He leaned back and indicated the laptop and box in front of me. "In there, you're going to find everything you need to become your sister. Did you think this was going to be as easy as just showing up and claiming to be Sybil?" He shook his head. "Come on, Hannah, you're smarter than that."

I inwardly cringed at his admonishment. To be honest, I hadn't considered the exact details of what would need to happen for me to assume Sybil's role. So yeah, in essence, I had thought I could just stroll into the conference, get what was needed, and get the fuck out of there. I didn't realize I'd need to give up my whole identity to do it. My dad's words from earlier in the morning came back to me, but I brushed the thought aside. He was wrong. This is what you did for someone you loved.

Rue picked up where she left off, not bothering to look at me as she plugged in some equipment and began tapping on the laptop. "To become Sybil Kelly, we're going to need to overlay your identity with hers. But to do that, Hannah Kelly can't exist anymore. Your identity and footprint are all over federal government records. If anyone gets any hint that you aren't who you say you are, all they'll need to do is run one quick background search, and bam, you're fucked harder than a porn star in a gang bang marathon."

My mouth gaped. I wasn't sure what shocked me more, the fact that she was right or that she might have a more foul and descriptive mouth than me. I turned to Simon. "Seriously, you gave me shit about my language, but you don't even bat an eye at that?"

Evan let out half a laugh, and I turned back towards him. "Si gave you the 'Ladies, don't curse.' speech, huh?" When I didn't say anything, he continued, "He tried to get Rue to clean up her language too, but as you can see, that didn't work out so well. He has a thing about women who swear. We're not sure if it's a kink or some other OCD tick he has."

I eyed Rue as she kept her eyes locked on the screen.

"Is that true? Did he also call you lass every 5 seconds and pin you up against walls against your will?"

She snorted and didn't look up. "Fuck no, that would be gross and perverted considering when he tried to get me to stop I was 13. But he did try the hot sauce on my tongue until he realized I was raised in a Cajun house and hot sauce is basically baby food to me."

"Great, why am I the lucky one, then? And wait, you've been working for him since you were 13?" Micheal, who until that moment had been so silent and still that I'd forgotten he was there, spoke up. The sound of his deep voice startled me so much that I jumped in my chair.

"You're not lucky. You've never been in more danger than you are right now and you'd better start remembering that. And how long Rue has been working for Simon is none of your business." It felt like someone threw a wet blanket over me. My previous trepidation and nervousness came back, but I didn't like the threatening way he chose to remind me of the position I was in. An inexperienced agent headed into the lion's den, surrounded by wolves.

"I'm pretty sure that I know exactly the kind of danger I'm in. Michael was it? But let me ask you, did you give that same warning to my sister before she signed her life away to this? Because I'm still not sure that your 'We would have seen it coming.' excuse is enough to convince me it did not somehow link her death to this mess."

He didn't smile, didn't blink, just continued to stare at me with that fiery intensity. Of his three counterparts, Micheal was the one who didn't bother to hide what was going on behind a mask of icy indifference. No, he hit you full-on with the force of his anger and rage. I just wasn't sure why I was the one on the receiving end of it. I was here to help them finish their job and get the bad guy. So why did it feel like the three of them would have rather worked next to a suicide bomber with an active bomb ticking away on his chest than me? What weren't they saying?

Simon's calf pressed more firmly against mine. "Hannah, I promise. We had nothing to do with Sybil's death, nor do we know who did. But I swear to you, lass, when this is all done, we will find them, and we will punish them." I stared into grey eyes surrounded by thick dark lashes that swirled with an unreadable emotion, letting my gaze drift over the hard set of his jaw, and after a moment, nodded slowly. I filed away the fact that he said, 'punish them' rather than bring them to justice, or catch them, for a later date. I didn't want to analyze that quip until I had time to process everything that was happening in front of me currently.

I felt his leg slowly withdraw from mine as he pushed away from the table and walked towards the cork-board, turning his back to our table. I instantly felt the absence of its warmth. Maybe it was just my imagination, but it felt like he had left it there on purpose as a silent sign of support. I took a deep breath and pulled the metal box towards me.

"Ok, I'm ready. What happens now?"

"Now," Rue drawled in her soft southern voice, "we say goodbye to Hannah and merge your biometric data with Sybil's."

"Wait, won't it be weird that Sybil's sister Hannah just vanished? What about birth records and everything? You can't erase the memory of sisters from a whole town."

"You're right, not much we can do if someone comes snooping around your old stomping grounds, but we're banking on anyone with an interest just looking at Sybil's file and not finding any discrepancies. So long as your fingerprints, biometrics, and all your previous files with the government are gone, that should be enough."

"So what, on paper, Hannah Kelly doesn't exist anymore and my parents never had me?" Rue nodded, frowning at something she was seeing on her screen. I was opening the box now and inspecting its contents. It looked like a passport, driver's license, and birth certificate. Everything I'd need to assume about Sybil's identity was there. It was creepy seeing my face, so similar to hers and yet different enough, next to her. I picked up her badge from Georgia Tech and held it up.

"Hold on now. You said nothing about actually going into her work. They're going to know right away I'm not Sybil."

Simon didn't turn around, just continued to stare at the map in front of him with his arms crossed. "You won't, but your badge will get you into the conference. You have to present credentials before you'll be allowed into some of the lectures and meetings you're expected to attend." I inwardly groaned. This is why I went into law enforcement. I liked to be active, moving outside. Nothing was worse than being stuck inside a dark room with some monotone voice droning on and on for hours. Was it too late to back out?

Something of my thoughts must have shown on my face, because Evan snatched the badge from my fingers and inspected it before dropping it back down into the box. "Too late to back out now, doll. But don't worry, I'm sure Simon will make sure you don't fall asleep in class."

"What does that mean? I thought I was going in on my own?" I eyed Simon's stiff back and when he said nothing, gave my attention back to the only two team members currently talking to me.

"Oh no, you're not going in alone. Didn't Simon tell you? He's your partner now. You'll need to maintain the level of relationship that Sybil and Simon shared, at least on the outside, to keep up the ruse you're really your sister. As of right now, you, Hannah, or should I say,

Sybil, are madly in love with your research counterpart, Dr. Gallagher."

Wait, what? "Are you joking? No way!" I stood up from the table and pointed in Simon's general direction. "First of all, I can't stand that man. He's insane. Second, I'm having a hard time even believing that Sybil had a relationship with him in the first place. Because," I looked over my should at the man in question who was now turned around and smirking at me, "no offense, but you're the type of guy Sybil was always warning me away from. She'd never be caught dead dating someone like you. So unless someone wants to cut the bullshit and tell me exactly what's going on. I'm doing this on my own or I'm out."

"Done!" Rue stood up excitedly, interrupting my little speech, and grinned around the room. "Phew! That was tough. I've never had so many files buried so deep or so effectively. For a minute I thought someone was trying to backdoor scrub everything on Sybil and make it so I couldn't get access, but I took care of that." She turned to me and pointed to the palm reader. "All that's left is for you to upload fresh prints and we're golden!" She seemed to notice the tension in the room and cleared her throat. "Did I miss something?"

Micheal took that moment to snort and dropped down onto the faded couch, crossing one long leg over the other. "Yeah, miss badass federal agent here was just explaining to us why Simon wasn't good enough for her precious sister."

I sputtered, "I never said not good enough, just that he wasn't her type. And the more I think about it, the more it makes sense. Sybil never dated, period. Her work was her life. Then all of a sudden you show up and it's nothing but Simon this and Simon that. So tell me, who's lying? My sister? Or you." I'd taken a few short steps to stand directly in front of Simon and cross my arms as I waited for him to answer me.

"Both, actually."

CHAPTER FIFTEEN

Hannah

The calm admission surprised me. I'd expected him to at least try to deny it a little. I was slightly shocked that he also lumped my sister in with the lie, though.

He met my stare, and I could swear I almost saw a gleam of admiration in it. Was he pleased I'd figure out their ruse? "You're right, Sybil and I weren't dating or in love. But we were working together. It was the only way our constant interactions weren't met with suspicion."

I thought back to the conversation with Sybil on her couch and how she'd been so dismissive of their relationship. It made sense now. "What do you mean, constant interactions? You clearly aren't a professor or scientist." If he was offended by the observation, he didn't say anything. "So exactly why did you go to so many lectures and classes with her?"

"Because I was trying to make connections through Sybil with the Abromov group. We were having trouble infiltrating their organization through other avenues. Your sister provided an opportunity, and we took it."

I looked around the room at the other three people who had remained silent, trying to gauge their reactions and whether I was getting the whole truth this time. They gave nothing away, though, just watched the exchange between Simon and me with predatory expressions. I had to remember that these people lied for a living, and no matter what truth I was presented with, there would always be layers to it.

"Okay. And you're saying that to continue with this mission, we have to keep the ruse up? That others knew about your fake relationship and will find it suspicious if we don't continue it?" I was genuinely flustered at the thought of having to pretend anything with Simon. "Can't we just break up or something?"

"What's the matter, princess, scared to be alone with me?" I wanted to wipe the cocky smirk off his face as the memory of us in the pitch-black hall made me blush.

"I am not afraid of you or anything else. I just don't see the point in pretending if we don't have to." I turned back around and stalked back to the table.

"The point," Evan spoke up now with a quick frown of admonishment towards Simon. "Is that everyone who had contact with your sister knew she was going to introduce a new member into the group. And despite their academic inclinations, scientists are notorious gossipers. The rumors had already spread that Sybil was in a relationship with Simon. We just didn't stop it."

Simon took a seat at the table again, this time across from me, thankfully. "It gave us the perfect cover to continue our meetings and also an added incentive to the group as to why Sybil was risking her career and pushing my acceptance so hard." The cocky smile was gone, a somber expression overcoming him. "You do out-of-character things for the ones you love."

I met his gaze and stayed quiet for a moment, thinking about everything they'd told me. Could they have been pretending to be in love to cover their agenda? It was plausible. Not likely, but plausible. Something still wasn't adding up, but until I had all the pieces in place, I would not be able to do much about it. For now, I needed to go along with their plan, if only to get closer to Simon, which was my goal. I just didn't want to get -that- close to him, especially since it seemed like every time I did all could think about getting him naked.

I turned to Rue, effectively dismissing Simon's presence. I may have to pretend to like him, but it didn't mean I had to start now. "Ok, beam me up then, Scotty." And held out my hand to her. For the first time, I saw her look at me with something other than suspicion.

"Oh, no fucking way! You're a Trekky?" She turned the scanner on and aligned my fingers and palm.

"Well, that depends. I guess you could say I'm a next-gen Trekky? My dad was a big fan. He took me to a couple of conventions when I was little."

"Well, that's all right then. At least you have some appreciation for the greatest work of televised fiction in the history of T.V." A low groan came from next to me and I turned to Evan, who was shaking his head with half a smile.

"Well, now you've done it. All she's going to talk about for the next hour is Picard that and Shatner this. It never bloody ends."

"Don't listen to him." Rue scoffed and turned back to her computer screen, typing away at more coding that was hard to make out. "His idea of good television is Netflix and chill with whatever bar bimbo he's picked up for the night."

Evan gave Rue what I thought was a genuine smile, the first I'd seen since I'd walked into the safe house. "Rue darling! Do I detect a little bit of jealousy? If you wanted to be my Netflix buddy, you just have to say so. I wasn't aware you enjoyed action movies." He wiggled his brows suggestively, and I saw a flash of a dimple as his grin widened. Holy hell, this man was stunning when he wasn't giving off serial killer vibes. I glanced from Rue to Evan, wondering if there was something more there than the teasing banter was suggesting. But Rue just kept her gaze glued to her screen, not even a hint of taking his bait in her features or voice.

"What I don't enjoy is the constant, 'Oh my goooosh, you're British? Say bloody hell for me.' or the "Ohhh, so have you like, actually met royalty?" I snickered at the way she mimicked the type of women Evan seemed to enjoy his alone time with. "Also, you are absolutely not my type E. Go use those dimples on someone who would fall for their lies." I almost didn't catch it. The flick of her honey-colored eyes was so subtle and quick that it almost seemed like it didn't happen. But for a moment I thought her gaze lingered on Micheal who was still sitting on the couch with his arms folded and his attention momentarily distracted by something on his phone.

Then Rue was standing and pulling my fingers away from the palm reader. Her face all serious business now. "All right, we're done. My job here is complete. Now it's on to phase two."

"Phase two?" I arched a brow and looked down at my hand, uncertain of what I should be feeling at the moment. I was now officially Dr. Sybil Kelly. My sister. I felt something like a heavy shadow settle around me, a darkness I couldn't quite explain. I thought taking this step in solving Sybil's murder would make me feel better somehow, but it only made me feel worse.

"Yes. The easy part is done. Now the hard work

begins, teaching you everything your sister would know." Simon was speaking now, and I watched as he nodded to Evan, who stood up and headed towards the light switch, flipping it and casting the room in the dim light from just the monitors on the far wall. A face popped up, and I instantly recognized it.

"That's Gregory Fischer," I said before anyone else could speak. "He is or was, a leading researcher and developer for the Army Research Lab. He went to Bucknell University and has a degree in mechanical engineering. Sybil's team worked with him on developing new, guided weapons systems." I flicked my gaze around the room when no one said a thing and noticed they were all staring at me again, much like they had been staring at me when I first walked in.

"And how exactly do you know this?" Simon asked casually, but I could sense a hidden weight behind it.

"You aren't the only one with connections or skills." I couldn't help but smirk, but quickly schooled my features into one that most of my colleagues at the agency would know. It was time this new team of mine learned I wasn't to be underestimated. "I've done profiling before. I know how to research my target and an organization. Once you told me who Sergei Abromov was, all it took was a few searches in the right places to start unraveling the connections."

I turned back around. "Next slide." A new face popped up at my command and I nodded. "That's Yolanda Dimitrov. She specializes in computer science and mechanical engineering. She's the one who developed the programming for some of the newest guidance systems for short-range ballistic missiles. Her lab is at the University of California, San Diego. Next slide."

Another face, another scientist, another person connected in some way to my sister, the Abromov group, and weapons systems development. There were seven in all and I could tell you their backgrounds, their degrees, even their favorite foods, and what color underwear they wore on Sundays. Well, maybe not that detailed, but I'd spent most of my night finding out as much information on the Abromov group as I could. Believe it or not, open-source information was one of the best ways to put together real-time intelligence on potential targets.

After I gave a brief overview of the very last scientist, I paused, noticing that Simon was staring at me in that intense way that made me think he was searching through the dark closets of my mind and detailing each and everything he found. I instantly thought of my dreams and Sybil. Jokes on you, buddy. My brain won't even let me into those closets. Doubt you'll have better luck.

Before the silence could become awkward, Simon

finally spoke, no hint of his thoughts in his tone or expression. "Well then, princess, since you've done your homework, let's move on to the next phase."

I couldn't help but feel some smug satisfaction. I'd managed to impress the badass international spy. Just call me Kelly, Hannah Kelly.

Simon

It was late in the evening and I could tell Hannah was thoroughly done, yet it wasn't us that insisted on continuing with the mission planning, it was her. She was tenacious and focused in a way that I had seen in only a few agents in the past. The ones that were so blinded by their objectives that it went beyond the scope of their jobs and pushed into obsession. They were the agents who had the dead eyes and emotionless gazes of souls who were lost until their last mission was complete. Convinced that if they could just get this one job done, they would be absolved of whatever dark thing that haunted them.

It only ever ended in one way: death. Either because they threw all caution and training to the wind, not caring if they lived or died just to achieve their goal. Often they preferred that it happened that way. Going down in a blaze of glory, righting one last wrong. Or someone like me was called in to silence them. Their carelessness led to mistakes, mistakes that would get other people, innocent people, killed. No matter which way it happened, it was suicide by mission. They knew what waited for them at the end.

"I don't care if you are Mario Andretti in a fucking 6 ft 5 muscle suit. There's no way you can get on target in time to get us out of there before shit hits the fan." Hannah was standing with her arms crossed under the red logo of her Thursday band shirt. I wasn't sure what I was more impressed with, the fact that she was talking to Micheal that way, or that he was taking it and hadn't snapped her neck yet. Somewhere in the past eight hours, she'd won some begrudging respect from the tall Italian from New York. I doubt she knew much about him, other than what he'd told her about his military background and piloting skills, but if she had realized she was speaking to the heir to one of the largest mafia families in the world, she might not be so willing to go toe to toe with him. She'd also probably arrest him on the spot.

"That's why you need to move your extraction point to here." Micheal jabbed a thick finger at the map that was pulled up on the screen. "It's only two more blocks, and there are plenty of pedestrians to cover your route. Rue will have the cameras taken care of and Evan will be ready with the distraction. Trust me, this is the best option."

Hannah frowned and I could tell she wanted to argue her point, but after a moment she brought her fingers to the bridge of her nose and sighed. "Fine, fine. You're the get-away expert, or whatever. If you say that's the best spot, then that's it." Her green eyes flashed when she opened them though and pinned him with a glare I was becoming all too familiar with, one that made me want to lose all restraint and kiss her senseless. "But I swear to God, your ass better be there. I am NOT planning on spending the rest of my life in some Swedish prison. They probably don't even have American TV or sports and I am not missing out on my Dawgs."

I stood and moved towards the map pulled up on the wall. It was covered with our notes and mission plans. This would be the last we would see it and everyone had spent the past few hours memorizing every detail. Once we left this room, Rue would scrub all the files clean and Evan and Micheal would destroy everything. Nothing would be left of our presence here. We would be gone, just like the ghosts we were.

"All right, we're good here. Mike, Evan, Rue, you know what to do." I gave each person a brief nod, and they returned it, understanding without me telling them what was required. "Hannah, it's time to go."

She looked like she wanted to balk at me, but then just sighed and rolled her eyes. "Fine, but I'm not going on your bike. That was enough torture for one lifetime. I'll call an Uber. Or..." She looked at the rest of the team hopefully, ".. can I catch a ride with one of you guys?"

I had to give her credit. She was resourceful. I had been mostly quiet during the mission planning, letting her take the lead, partly to see how good she would be at it and also to allow her to have some sense of control. It was a false sense though because for the few hours she'd been going over details with Micheal, Evan, and Rue, we'd spent triple that creating the plan in the first place. Nothing was left to chance. Not even her.

"Sorry princess, you won't get any help from them." Green eyes shot daggers at me and I couldn't stop the smirk that crept up. "But if you behave, we don't have to take the bike."

"Fucking neanderthal men..." she muttered under her breath, but sighed. "Fine, I'm too tired to argue. As long as it's not on the back of that damn bike, you can take me home." The fact that she'd said it like she was the Queen of England made me almost laugh out loud. When was the last time someone made me smile or laugh outside of my team? I couldn't remember and for some reason, the fact that the hellion in ripped jeans and some obscure band t-shirt was the one who made it happen bothered me in a way I wasn't ready to think about yet.

My life's work revolved around limiting the ties and connections I had to the outside world. Other than the three other people in this room, I had no one to call family or friends. The last time I'd allowed someone to get close to me in any way, they'd ended up on the receiving end of my silencer. The fallout from that entanglement had nearly cost me my life and put the rest of my team in jeopardy of being dragged down with me. I wouldn't risk them again.

As Hannah went down the stairs and stepped out onto the dark street in front of me, I placed a hand on the small of her back and guided her towards the side alley where Evan's car would be parked. He'd take my Triumph back to the penthouse where the rest of the team would wait for our own debriefing. After the hallway incident and the way she'd surprised us all with her intelligence gathering, I knew they were going to have more questions and concerns. Frankly, so did I.

I opened the door to Evan's dark gray Audi coupe and noticed she'd stopped to stare at the car. "Something wrong with your chariot, princess?"

She flicked her eyes back to me and shook her head. "No, I'm just starting to think that maybe I went into the wrong line of work. Being a spy seems to pay well."

"We work hard and play harder. Evan likes his toys." I shut the door as she climbed in and moved around to the driver's side.

"Yeah?" She wasn't looking at me, more interested in inspecting the car's interior. "And what do you like?"

I wanted to say a green-eyed brunette with lips made for sinning and an ass that made my mouth water, but I didn't. Instead, I just grunted and pulled out into the dark Atlanta night. "Nothing. I should have said they work hard and play harder. I don't have time for hobbies."

She scoffed and leaned back, closing her eyes with a contented smile on her face. "Well, you're missing out. I could get used to this kind of playing. These seats are fucking amazing. I'm never getting on your bike again."

It was my turn to scoff as the Audi shifted and responded to my commands. "I can guarantee you, princess, nothing compares to being seated on a powerful engine and taking control. There's freedom in it."

"You mean freedom to fall off and die? No thanks."

I smirked, and the car lurched forward, responding the way only a high-performance sports car can. We flew down the expressway with the city lights blurring by. "No, there's freedom in pushing yourself just to the edge of chaos and in trusting in yourself. Trusting that you are the one in complete control. In letting the part of you that fears danger and death have just a taste. Then, at the last minute, pulling back from the razor's edge. It's addicting."

I looked over, her lips were parted, her eyes shining bright in the dim car interior and for a moment I thought I saw longing or desire reflected there. The same longing and desire echoed inside my own soul. Then her eyes shuttered again, and she turned away to look out her window.

"This isn't the way to my apartment."

"Aye."

"Where are we going?"

"You're Sybil Kelly now. You're going to your townhome."

CHAPTER SIXTEEN

Hannah

He'd pulled up to my sister's townhome where I was still expecting there to be crime scene tape and evidence markers scattered around, but instead, it looked as if nothing had ever happened. As if last week's chaos was just a distant memory or a bad dream.

"What is this?" I turned to look at Simon, but he was getting out of the car and coming around to my side to open my door. I looked up at him in confusion and anger. Why had he brought me here? My heart beat faster with fear. Was he going to hurt me? Had he hurt Sybil?

"You need to get out of the car and pretend we just came back from a date, Sybil." His voice was pitched low so that only I could hear him, but the way he emphasized my sister's name made me think that someone was there

I couldn't see. My eyes darted to the empty street and parking spaces.

"Simon I'm not getting out of this car until you tell me what the fu-" His low warning of "Language.." stopped me. That's right, Sybil would never swear. ".. what the heck is going on?"

"Come on darling, I know you're tired, but we need to get you inside. Big week ahead of us." Simon pulled the door wider and held out his hand, silently demanding that I follow his lead. Reluctantly, I put my hand in his and allowed him to pull me out onto the open street. As we walked side by side, he leaned his head down, mouth in my ear. "You're officially Sybil Kelly now, which means Sybil is no longer dead. If the person or people who wanted to harm your sister figure out that you're posing as her, you'll be targeted as well." I gasped at the real-ization.

"But you said that you weren't aware of any threats on Sybil's life, that you didn't know who was responsible!" He squeezed my arm and growled in my ear again, "Keep your voice down. YOU are Sybil now, do you understand? And I don't know who killed Sybil. But I'm not going to take the chance that it wasn't someone out to target her for her work with Abromov and risk them going after you, too. So long as they think they see Sybil here, then they'll assume the hit didn't go as planned and she's alive, leaving you alone."

He was pushing me up the short flight of stairs to Sybil's front entrance, but I turned as we reached the door and stopped. "Simon, I can't. I can't go in there." I didn't want to see the scene where my sister's body lay broken and bloody. Or envision where she'd been, how she'd fought, as the life was beaten out of her.

His eyes softened just a little bit of understanding. "It's ok. I took care of it."

"What do you mean? They only processed the scene four days ago. There's no way it's been cleaned yet."

"It's all gone, Hannah..." He let my name slip from his lips quietly, probably realizing that calling me Sybil right now would not be the best way to calm me down. "Everything. I promise there is nothing in there that will remind you of her. The 911 calls, the evidence, everything has been quietly scrubbed and put away until after we complete this mission."

I couldn't believe what I was hearing. He'd gotten rid of the evidence? Her death was just non-existent anymore? As I stared at him in the growing silence, I realized that his comment in the car about his work being his playtime was utterly truthful. This man lived and breathed his mission. Because there was no way that a death as violent and gruesome as my sisters would have been just tossed into the back corner of a file room to be dusted off at a later date.

"How long have you been planning this?" I

murmured, trying not to let the rage I felt boiling just under the surface show in my tone.

"Not as long as you're suspecting of me right now. I mean it. I had nothing to do with your sister's death. But the minute I left your office on Friday, I began to get the records sealed and evidence locked away. I knew then that you'd be the key to helping me." He didn't offer an apology or even show an ounce of remorse for his deception.

"You manipulated me."

He cocked his head and leaned in closer, those dark eyes boring into mine, and his scent, like pine and leather, washed over me. "Did I? Or did I give you exactly what you were looking for, Princess?"

"I told you not to call me princess, or lass, or any other name. It's just Ha-"

"Tsk, tsk, not anymore, it's not, Sybil now, and we just came back from a date. Do you know what happens at the end of a date?" There was a sinister glint in the gray depths that made me gasp, but before I could get another word out, his lips were covering mine and the desire that crashed through me shocked me. My hands sunk into the wood frame as I tried to brace myself and resist the overwhelming urge to cling to him.

His kiss was exactly like he was. Controlled, thorough, demanding. There was no roughness or overly rushed sloppiness in the way he coaxed my lips apart and slid our tongues together.

The taste of him was intoxicating and before I knew it, I was arching into him as primal need flooded through me. If this is what he meant about riding the razor's edge of chaos and control, then he was right. It was addicting. *He* was addicting, and everything in me wanted to jump off that ledge to see exactly what would happen if I gave in.

A dark groan escaped his lips, "That's it, princess, just let go."

Alarm bells started to go off in my brain, though, just as I was about to fall into the haze of lust. I couldn't let him trap me like this. He might be entirely focused on his mission, but so was I. And no good could come from this. It would be a relief to scratch the itch between us, but as he'd already told me, there wasn't any room for anything other than his mission in his life. There definitely wasn't room for me. And I didn't want there to be. I had to guard my heart and my own mission. The click of the doorknob under my palm brought the clarity I needed and just as he was sliding his hand under the hem of my shirt, I turned it and let the door swing open, throwing us off balance and into my sister's front entrance.

"What the fu-" He growled but caught himself. His grey eyes looked black in the dim light and for a moment

I felt fear rising along with the lust. But not that he would hurt me. No, this time the only fear I had was of losing myself in him and never being able to regain control.

"Don't ever do that–" I was cut off by the gun that he pulled from his waistband and the silencer that he swiftly attached to it. "Excuse—" He brought his finger to his to be quiet as I was pushed behind him and against the wall, stopping my questions. Real, genuine fear crept up my spine now as I peered past him and into the darkened living room. With a silent gesture, he indicated that I needed to stay put, and I nodded, understanding. I had no weapon to help, and he needed to clear the town-home. Following him would be foolish if there was someone in there who shouldn't be. I made a mental note not to leave without my weapon next time. It had been stupid of me to forget it in the first place. But then I remembered why I'd been so distracted at the time and immediately became angry at him all over again.

He disappeared into the darkness and I waited in the silence for what seemed like forever, but I knew it was only mere seconds. And then he was back and flicking the hall light on.

"It's clear." His face was unreadable. A dark shadow settled across it and he didn't put his gun away.

"I take it the door wasn't supposed to be unlocked?" When he shook his head, I nodded and moved just a few feet into the living room. It was empty, with no furniture, no rug, no bloodstains. It was like my sister had never been there at all.

"I found this, though." Turning around, I frowned as he held something out and then felt an icy wave of dread wash over me. It was a brown paper bag with my name written on it.

I swallowed past the lump in my throat but didn't reach out to take it from him. "Did - did you open it up?" When he shook his head yes, I inwardly sighed with relief. That meant it couldn't be that terrible. But Simon was watching me intently as he reached in the bag and pulled out a single polaroid picture, handing it over to me. It was shadowy and shaky, like the person who took it had shaken it too much or too fast before it dried. My frown deepened as I stared at it, trying to make out what it was. It looked like a close-up of grass covered in shadows and at the bottom of the white box were the words, "Don't forget your promise."

CHAPTER SEVENTEEN

Hannah

I pulled the brush through my hair one last time before setting it down on the bathroom counter in my hotel room. The past 48 hours had been a blur and full of tension. Simon and I had barely spoken to each other since the incident at Sybil's townhome. Not that I was complaining. The memory of his kiss still lingered, leaving me feeling on edge and unsettled. But it wasn't as bad as the way the picture that had been left behind made me feel. Every time I looked at it, my stomach turned to knots and I felt nauseated.

Finishing the last touches on my make-up, I took a long look in the mirror and sighed. It was as good as it was going to get. The dark circles under my eyes couldn't be helped. Nights of hazy dreams where I woke up in cold sweats had meant that sleep was elusive. Not to mention the jet lag from the long hours of travel as we made our way from Atlanta to Stockholm. Sybil would have never looked so tired and ragged. "Remember your promise."

I couldn't be sure that it was Sybil who had written the note or taken the picture. But the brown bag with my name on it was all too familiar, even if it was only a dream I remembered it from. Who else would have left it? Who else would know about a dream if that's all that it was? Just like every time I tried to remember anything at all about the bag, I felt my heart start to race and my limbs began to shake. Evan had said I was having a panic attack and that maybe it was best not to push my brain so hard to remember. That when it was ready, it would come back to me.

After the townhome was cleared and we were certain no one else was in the vicinity, Simon had notified the team about the possibility of someone being there and the present they had left me. They'd decided it was best that I didn't go back to my apartment, and that's how I'd ended up staying in a guest room in their penthouse. After they'd processed the bag and photo for any prints, which there were none, Evan had put me through some memory recall drills to try to jog something. But just like now, my body had refused to allow me to unlock whatever my brain was hiding.

I bowed my head and took some slow deep breaths,

counting back from 100. After I'd nearly passed out from hyperventilating, Evan stopped trying to push me and taught me some techniques to get past the panic before it took control. I gripped the bathroom counter tighter as the darkness around my vision slowly faded away and frustration took over. Why was I reacting this way? Why couldn't I remember? Why did I feel like my sister had all the secrets and answers, but all I had were questions? Before I could dive deeper into that train of thought and start the panic all over again, I heard a knock.

Checking the peephole and opening the door revealed Simon outside of it and I forgot all thoughts of dark secrets as I devoured the sight of the man in front of me.

He didn't look like he'd been traveling for almost two days straight, or spent hours reviewing details and plans for our mission tomorrow night. Gone was the plain t-shirt, dark leather jacket, and faded jeans that blended him in so well among the crowds. Instead, he was dressed like he just walked off the Cambridge campus as every college girl's hot professor fantasy. A dark grey blazer over a navy blue knit sweater and crisp white dress shirt stretched across a wide chest and defined shoulders. Matching grey slacks that showed off muscular thighs and Italian loafers completed the look, but it was the gold-framed glasses he adjusted on the bridge of his nose that had me drooling. First, it was the clean shaved jaw, and now it's glasses. If he shows up with a pipe and ascot next, I may have an actual heart attack.

When he cleared his throat and arched a brow over the rim of those glasses, I realized I'd been staring without saying anything much longer than was polite and I felt my face flush with embarrassment. "Sorry, just the glasses…" I waved a limp hand in his direction and immediately wanted to slap it over my mouth and hide in shame. Really Hannah? The glasses? "I mean, I just haven't seen you wear them before. I'll grab my coat and purse." I turned back into my room as fast as I could, but not before I caught the hint of a smirk flicker at the corner of his lips.

When I stepped back out into the hall, the smirk was gone and his eyes held a glimmer of amusement to them, but he remained silent. Tilting my chin up, I walked stiffly towards the elevator and tried not to think about how I'd basically turned into a "dim-witted ninny" as my Memaw would say, over a guy who knew how to wear a suit. There are a ton of men back home in Atlanta who look good in suits. If that's what I like, and oh boy do I like, I'll just go home and find one.

We stepped inside the elevator and as it closed with a soft whoosh; I looked inside my purse to pull out the badge that would identify me as one of the conference attendees and allow us access to the lecture we were on the way to.

"I don't wear glasses." His deep voice rolled over me in a delicious wave, the soft Scottish lilt just barely accenting his words. After hardly hearing him talk for the past two days, it felt like gasoline was thrown on the flame of my libido. Suddenly, every part of me wanted to melt into a puddle on the floor at his feet and beg to hear him speak again. My tongue felt like glue, but I somehow managed to squeak out an "Oh." as I blinked at him. Great, back to being the dim-witted ninny. Sorry, Memaw.

"It's for the disguise. People tend to view a man wearing glasses as non-threatening." The sinister grin he threw at me was a complete contradiction to his words. "But it's good to know you like them, princess. I'll have to remember that." Was that a wink I caught as he stepped out of the now-open elevator doors and into the hotel lobby? Did Simon Gallagher just wink at me?

By the time my jaw was picked up off the floor and Memaw's lectures about my lack of brain cells had raced through my brain, the doors were almost closing and I had to slam my hand between them to keep from getting stuck inside.

"Hannah?" A male voice, full of surprise, caught my attention, but I couldn't be sure they were speaking to me. I was Sybil here and in a foreign country like this, didn't think it was possible for anyone to recognize me. "Hannah Kelly?" The man was insistent now and as I turned away from the elevator towards the sound, I saw a handsome gentleman approaching me. He looked vaguely familiar, with a broad, friendly face and light brown hair. I frowned, trying to place where I knew him from, but realized I had to quickly cover and get into character. I wasn't Hannah, I was Sybil.

"I'm sorry, you must be mistaken. I'm not Hannah." I smiled brightly at the man and looked over his shoulder for Simon, who was watching the exchange intently but didn't make a move to step in.

"What?" The man frowned and moved closer, confusion and a hint of anger in his gaze. "You've got to be kidding me. I know it wasn't the most "impressive performance" you'd ever seen, but really? You're going to pretend like you don't even know me? It's Dennis." His tone dripped with disdain, and he crossed his arms. I couldn't help but think he looked like a schoolteacher scolding a child, and then suddenly I knew where I recognized him from. He was Dennis from the dating app I'd briefly joined about a year ago. It had been after another failed office romance and I'd sworn off dating any other co-workers. I could only take so many "It's not you, it's me." lines just to find out they requested reassignment or quickly moved on to their next conquest and never spoke to me again. It didn't take a genius to figure out that it was definitely me in the romance equation, so I'd decided to try a different approach. Dennis had seemed like a nice, safe bet. He was a teacher at Georgia Tech, not in Sybil's field, but just a plain old English major. We'd hit it off right away through messages and I thought we'd had a real connection. But then the night we were supposed to meet, he'd never shown up, and I'd gone home to another takeout container and all night Vampire Diaries marathon.

Still, it didn't matter. The way he was speaking and the attention he was drawing to me had to end. I could unravel the mystery of what he was talking about later, but right now, I had to get to the lecture with Simon. "I'm sorry. I think you're mistaking me for my sister. I'm Dr. Sybil Kelly, not Hannah." The lie tasted like acid on my tongue and I hated even saying it, but I couldn't stop now, and something about the way he was leering at me made me want to defend myself just a little. "And I think I know who you are. Hannah mentioned a date that stood her up. I'm assuming that was you?" I arched a brow and gave him a long head-to-toe once over, hoping to convey as much of Sybil's cold ice-queen judgemental expression.

"Well, that makes sense. No way Hannah would be here for the convention. But stood her up?" His voice was getting louder, and I saw Simon begin to slowly make his way across the lobby towards us. I needed to end this fast.

"I didn't stand her up. She showed up at my apartment the night of our date practically naked, claiming she couldn't wait. But I'm not surprised that's what she told you. I'm sure she didn't want her precious "Sissy" to know just what a little freak she was."

I stood there, too shocked and angry to speak. Just what the hell was he talking about? Dennis leaned in closer, his face flushed red with fury, and jabbed a finger directly at my chest. "You tell your slut sister that she needs to delete those pictures she took and that if she ever comes near me again, I'm filing charges. I don't care what government agency she works for. Blackmail is a federal crime."

Simon's deep voice was dark and deadly as he slid silently behind Dennis. "I would suggest you remove your finger from Dr. Kelly's chest before you find it removed from you."

Dennis looked up at Simon, who towered a good four to five inches above him, and balked slightly, taking half a step back. But he didn't lose his venomous tone as he redirected his gaze back to me. "I mean it. I have a fiancé in the biochemistry department now. We are here together. And I've already told her everything about what happened. I don't have any reason to be afraid of those images getting out now and frankly, I realized it was her kinks, not mine, to be ashamed of. Either she gets rid of everything, or I'm filing charges. I just might do it, anyway." Then he turned around and stalked away to where a petite blonde woman with a concerned expression was waiting for him by the concierge station.

Simon looked at me with his familiar, unreadable mask in place. "Is there something you'd like to tell me?"

I shook my head and let out half a laugh in disbelief. "Are you kidding me? I have no freaking clue what he's talking about. HE stood ME up. And blackmail? Pictures? KINKS!?" I was trying to whisper, but it was hard in the open lobby with its tall ceilings and shiny marble floors. Everything seemed to echo and more than a few eyes turned toward us. Great, add "pervert" to my long list of desirable traits.

Simon pulled open the hotel door and ushered me out to where Micheal was waiting with our vehicle.

I felt him bend his head down to my ear as his hand pressed on the small of my back, guiding me towards a blacked-out Mercedes. "Yes, let's talk about kinks. I'm very interested in that topic." He opened the door as I sputtered, "I do not have kinks!"

Micheal glanced back at us in the rearview mirror. "Hannah has kinks? What kind? Bondage? Spanking? Roleplay?"

It felt like my entire body was now on fire with embarrassment. "I absolutely do not have kinks and if I did, I would not discuss them with you-" I glared at Michael and then turned to Simon as he slid into the back seat next to me, "Or you!"

Michael snickered and pulled out onto the street. "Oh, everybody has some sort of kink or thing they're into when it comes to sex. You just might not have discovered yours yet." Dark brown eyes flickered to mine, dancing with amusement. "I'm going to guess yours is spanking. But you'll never know if you don't try it." He gave me a slow, lazy grin that would absolutely wreck any other woman within a five-mile radius. "What do you say, Hannah, want to figure it out?"

"That is -not- happening Michael Galliano. I'll break every joint in your hand if you even think about it. You'll never be able to jack off properly again for the rest of your life." Micheal let out a barking laugh and continued to maneuver through the busy streets towards the convention center.

"You're right." Simon's voice slivered through the dimly lit back seat, and I turned to look at him. "Micheal won't be the one to learn all your dirty secrets." I sucked in a breath as he leaned in and brushed a piece of lint from my blouse, those gunmetal grey eyes never leaving mine. "Why?" I breathed, not sure if I wanted to know the answer.

"Because I will."

CHAPTER EIGHTEEN

Hannah

"Because I will."

Who knew that three words could cause such a rippling wave of nervous excitement and dread to fill me? They certainly weren't the three words that I ever expected to be playing over and over in my head. Yet here I was, trying not to view the side profile of the man next to me as we stood to exit from our third and final lecture of the day, with those words on repeat.

What I had expected to be a long and boring day filled with faking my way through discussions I'd had no clue about had ended up being rather enjoyable. Somehow, Simon knew enough of the subjects to be able to hold the conversation just long enough to be deemed polite before he would whisk me away on some pretense of needing to speak to another attendee. On top of that, his low voice kept up a running commentary on the presentations in such an insightful and simple way that I found myself genuinely interested in some of the subjects. Now and then he'd make a quip that would catch me off guard and I'd find myself snickering behind my brochure, much to the disapproving stare of the serious scientists we were surrounded by.

He was warm; he was polite, and he was an absolute gentleman. Nothing at all like the domineering, arrogant, and personal space-invading man he'd been ever since I'd met him. It was what I'd thought he'd be like to begin with, when I thought he wore an ascot and not a leather jacket. So why was it that with his hand on the small of my back, guiding me through the crowded conference room, was I only thinking about the intense way he'd cornered me? Why did all the spots he placed small, innocent touches throughout the day make me want to see the facade ripped away to reveal the Simon underneath?

Maybe it was the fact that both of us were exhausted from the full day of pretense, or maybe we both felt the weight of the evening's mission fast approaching, but the car ride back to our hotel was mostly silent. Simon hadn't gotten into the backseat with me and I was happy to have the chance to have some space and just think. While Evan and Simon rode together in the front seat, talking softly to each other, I mulled over the mission, going over the meticulous plans that would go into effect in just a few hours. Walking through every step helped ease the confusion and settle my thoughts over Simon. I turned my gaze from the dark head of the man who'd been occupying far too much space in my brain to the window and the city streets that were awash in the late afternoon sun. The KTH Royal Institute of Technology was a beautiful campus with red brick buildings and stone pathways surrounded by lush green lawns and sculpted topiaries. It was a unique mix of old-world European styles and modern minimalism.

There had been a moment when I'd walked next to Simon towards the main entrance and had paused on the cobblestones in front of a circular fountain that I'd felt like this was a surreal experience. Just a few days ago I'd mockingly called myself a Bond girl and now I was in Europe and neck deep in a dangerous international espionage plot. My stomach gave a nervous flip, and I nearly dropped the brush in my hand as a knock sounded on my hotel room door. So much for being a cool, calm, collected international spy. I couldn't even maintain control of my brush.

I opened the door to a grinning Rue who was dressed like she'd just stepped out of an urban fantasy book cover, complete with tight leather electric blue pants and a black mid-drift t-shirt that said 'Let's get wicked!'. I was more than a little jealous of her sense of style and had already decided that if we ever got close enough, I was dragging her with me on a shopping spree in the hopes that some of it would rub off on me. I moved to the side as she brushed past me with a grin carrying what looked like a black garment bag and a cosmetics case.

"What's all this?" I shut the door and spun around to see her hanging up the garment bag and then unzipping it to reveal a gold sequined gown that glittered like treasure in the setting sunlight that streamed in from my windows.

My mouth dropped a little as I moved towards the dress, fingers hesitantly reaching out to touch the shimmering fabric. When I'd told Simon that I'd needed time to go dress shopping for the party tonight, he'd just shook his head and said not to worry about it. I thought he'd meant that what I'd packed would be formal enough, making me think that the event tonight was less about getting dressed up and more about the mission. I couldn't have been more wrong. This gown looked like it had graced the cover of a fashion magazine. It looked exactly like something Sybil would have chosen.

At the thought of my sister wearing something so sumptuous, my fingers flinched, and I withdrew them, frowning.

"I can't wear this Rue. This is way too fancy for me."

She just shrugged and went about setting out makeup products on the little desk that was serving as my vanity.

"Not my call, cher. Si says to dress you up like a golden Cinderella, so that's what you'll be." She turned and gave me a wink. "Just no turning into a pumpkin at midnight."

I scoffed and rolled my eyes. "Cinderella" was my code name for this mission. No thanks to Evan. When I'd objected profusely to Simon using "Princess", Evan had popped up with "How about Cinderella?" And then every single one of them had latched on to the idea, choosing names based on the iconic movie for themselves. It had been so funny listening to Evan and Micheal argue over who was going to be Gus Gus that I'd forgotten to be upset or even ask what Simon's codename was. When I'd remembered a little while later and had questioned him, he'd just smirked and ignored me.

"So what, Simon is the Fairy Godmother?"

Rue barked out a laugh and motioned me to sit down.

"Hah! If you consider him the fairy godmother of shit attitudes and overbearing psychopaths, then yeah, he can be your fairy godmother." I smiled, glad that she was helping me get ready tonight and that I wouldn't have to do it on my own. I was terrible at the girly stuff that always seemed to come naturally to Sybil. More than that, I was glad to finally get the chance to probe her a little deeper about her relationship with said "fairy godmother of shit attitudes", something I wholeheartedly agreed with.

"It sounds like you and I are on the same page with

him. So what gives? Why do you work for him?" I closed my eyes as she went in with black eyeliner and felt the cool felt tip glide against my skin.

"Going to try to use some of those famous fed profiling techniques on me?" Her voice was light, but I could hear a hard edge underneath. Rue definitely had some history with the FBI, one that I was sure I wouldn't find any information about if I tried to look.

"No. I'm just curious. You don't exactly strike me as the type of woman to hang around someone who is as, "I hesitated, trying to find the right word to describe Simon's intensity and finally just settled on calling a spade a spade. "..assholeish as Simon seems to be."

She went quiet for a moment and when I opened my eyes; I found her staring intensely at me. It wasn't until I glanced down that I realized she had a small but sharp blade held so delicately against the vein of my throat that I'd barely felt it there. Her voice when she spoke was low and cold.

"Mon cher. I know you think you might know me. You think I might be the weak link in Simon's armor? But I can assure you, I am not."

It took every ounce of training I had to not show fear. No matter how human these people seemed, they were not. They were killers, even Rue, with her electric blue leather pants and amazing sense of style.

My voice was just as low and quiet as hers when I

replied and I was proud of myself for how little it shook as I said, "I don't think you're the weak link, Rue. I don't even know what to think. I just want to know more about the man who I'm supposed to be trusting my life with. About the man who my sister trusted her life with."

We stared at each other for a few heartbeats more before she slowly drew the knife away and it disappeared as if by magic, back into whatever pocket she had been hiding it. I couldn't help the shuddering breath I let out as she turned back to the makeup on the table and selected what looked like an eyeshadow palette and began blending colors onto a blush.

"Simon saved me when the FBI wanted to put a minor away for the rest of her life for just trying to save her parents."

I wanted to interrupt and argue that the agency wouldn't even bother with juvenile crimes, but the gleam of her knife flashed in my mind and thought better of it.

"What do you mean?" I lowered my lashes as she leaned forward with the makeup brush, although not completely, I wouldn't be caught off guard again.

The soft tip of the brush glided over my lids as she spoke. "I wasn't exactly the most popular kid in school. When I was six, I could write and code like most kids could read those First Little Reader books every elementary teacher has." She turned back to the makeup and began blending two different foundation colors.

"It helped that my papa was a computer programmer for LSU and my mama was an engineer." She dabbed my cheeks with the makeup sponge, her hazel eyes going distant, her accent getting thicker as she spoke. "They immigrated from Mali when I was a baby to New Orleans. But being new to America, they fell in with the wrong crowd."

She set the sponge down and began to filter through the rest of the palettes on the table, finally choosing a soft golden bronzer and a large brush. "My papa was in debt to some people. The mob, or mafia. I'm not really sure. But they came to collect their money one day and when Papa didn't have it, they tried to make him steal it."

"What did they want him to do?" Rue brushed the bronzer over my cheekbones and sighed.

"The tête de *noeud*, 'dickheads'... "She spat the French insult out as if it burned her tongue. "thought that because my papa was good with computers, he could somehow get past bank encryption and make them some easy money." Her full lips curled down at the memory. "He tried to tell them it was more complicated than that, that he was just a simple programmer who updated servers and kept teachers able to enter their students' grades. But they wouldn't listen."

She moved from her spot at the table and went to the closet where the dress was hanging and pulled it down. "You can probably guess what happened next. When he

didn't do what they wanted, they threatened my mama."
She shook her head. "My papa, he was so scared, he told
them he would do it, but he didn't even know where to
start. He would have made a mess of everything. So I did
it. I hacked into the State Bank and Trust Co and stole
the money."

My mouth dropped open with the causal way she
spoke as she laid out the gown and pair of gold thong
heels on the bed. "Rue, how old were you?"

"I was thirteen."

My heart lurched, and I felt tears well. At thirteen
years old, I was chasing Sybil around our front yard with
a frog I'd found in our neighbors' pond, not hacking into
bank accounts to save my parents from getting murdered
right in front of me. I swallowed the emotions down and
turned my back to her to pull the gown over my hips.

"How much money did you transfer?"

She laughed and helped me with the zipper once I'd
pulled the thin straps over my shoulders. "Ahh yes, how
much money is always the question, isn't it? It was three
million dollars."

I whirled around, my eyes wide with shock as recognition dawned on me. "Rue! Are you telling me the
largest bank heist in the history of the United States was
done by a thirteen-year-old girl?"

A small smile sad smile turned the corners of her lips
up and she shrugged. "Oui. I'm the Fleur de Lis."

CHAPTER NINETEEN

Rue was the Fleur de Lis. I was in the room with a literal criminal legend. We'd done some case studies in school on how the mastermind of the greatest cybercrime in the history of the United States had gotten away with stealing so much money at once and not get caught. But never in any of the text had they mentioned that it had been a thirteen-year-old little girl.

I shook my head in disbelief. "Rue, the Fleur de Lis was never caught. Not trying to call you a liar, chica, but why in the world would the FBI have let you go if they had you? It's been a huge stain on the reputation of the bureau for years."

And it was true, every couple of years Dateline or some other criminal investigation show would tease that they had finally uncovered the potential identity of the Fleur de Lis, and a flood of new tips would come in. Old agents were interviewed, and the entire fiasco would unfold again.

She shrugged and gathered up the makeup that was scattered around the table. I sat down on the edge of the bed and pulled on the strappy gold heels, noting appreciatively that they weren't so high that I wouldn't be able to run in them if needed.

"That's where Simon came in."

"When I hacked the bank, I didn't understand that the gang leader wouldn't know how to access the money." She sighed and sat down on the bed next to me. "I wasn't good at covering it up either. I knew all the principles, I understood the code, and I knew I could do it. I just didn't have the experience to know how to cover my tracks."

I waited patiently for her to continue, watching her as her fingers drummed absentmindedly on the slick leather of her pants as if they were flying over the keys at her computer.

"It didn't take long for the bank to figure out what had happened and for the FBI to show up at the door. But by then it was too late. The gang leader had realized he couldn't get access to his money, and he came looking for someone to blame."

Rue turned towards the window where the sun had almost completely set over Stockholm and I watched as the memories and the ghosts of her past played across her face. "I didn't know Hannah. I was just trying to save my parents. But it didn't matter. They died anyway because I thought I could outsmart a stupid gangster." She took a deep shuddering breath and stood up quickly to finish gathering her things. "When the FBI came and realized that it was a thirteen-year-old girl who had committed the crime, not a thirty-something programmer at LSU, they didn't know what to do with me. The money couldn't be returned because turns out, no one could get past the encryption I'd layered it in. Not even me. The backdoor access key I'd created was corrupted, and the money was lost forever."

"But how did Simon save you? What did the FBI do?" I sat there in bewilderment as I tried to think of what I would do if I'd been the agent assigned to the case and had realized that such a huge crime had been pulled off by a minor. More importantly, a now orphaned little girl, because it sounded like her parents had been killed right in front of her for something she had no control over.

She smiled softly and sat back down again, turning to face me this time, her amber eyes swimming with emotion. "The FBI didn't know what to do with me. I was a minor who had committed, knowingly, a major federal crime. But my parents were dead, and I didn't have any other legal guardians or representation. Not to mention they couldn't access the money." She snorted and flicked a piece of lint off her pants. "And trust me, they tried. They kept me in a room for days, making me run every code and program I knew. They put me up against the best cyber security teams they could find, hoping that either I would break it first or they would." Her voice took on a hard edge. "They didn't care. My parents were dead. They didn't care that I was only thirteen. Or that if I could have, I would have already had access to the money because it would have saved their lives. They just wanted it back and then they'd figure out what to do with me."

"I thought I'd never leave that room. I slept and ate there for days. Finally, someone must have realized that they couldn't treat a thirteen-year-old girl like that and brought me some clothes. A child psychologist came to make sure I was," she raised her fingers and mimicked a quote, "Mentally viable enough to be interrogated."

I didn't know what to think. Never in my years as an agent had I ever heard of so many misdoings and procedural fuck ups in an investigation. I didn't know who had been the office chief at the time of Rue's detainment, but I wanted to punch him or her right in the face. What Rue was describing was torture, plain and simple. Torture of a thirteen-year-old child. It made me sick to my stomach to think about it. No wonder she'd hated me right away. I represented the people who did that to her.

"When the interrogator came in, he knew right away that the whole situation was a giant cluster-fuck." Rue paused for a moment as if she was carefully contemplating her next words, or perhaps reliving the hell she'd suffered through. "That interrogator was Simon."

Somehow out of the whole story, that was the one piece of information that made sense. The idea that the bureau was knowingly detaining and interrogating a minor didn't sit right with me. If the news had gotten out, then shit really would have hit the fan and if there was one thing I knew about the FBI, they protected their reputation at all costs. To bring in an outside entity to do their dirty work only made sense.

"Simon convinced the FBI it would be in their best interest to release me into his custody and to chalk the money up as lost forever. That's what the bank has insurance for, after all." She stood up from the bed and gave a small shudder, as if she was visibly shaking off the memory of her horrific ordeal. "I also think he promised to have me try to find a way to access it because periodically I get sent encryption keys to break and reprogram. But, to my knowledge, it hasn't been done yet."

I stood up as well, startled by a knock at the door but ignored it, so enamored with her story that I forgot all about my mission and the event in just a short while. "So what happened? You just went to live with a trained mercenary for hire and now you work for him? He's your adoptive dad or something?"

Rue smiled and gave a half shrug. "I prefer to think of

him as an annoyingly overprotective brother. The dad role doesn't suit him." The knock sounded again, a little louder and more insistent. I knew it was Simon, but I also felt I needed to hear the rest of this story before seeing the man himself.

Glancing at the door, Rue turned back around to me, grabbing both my hands in hers and holding them tightly. The intensity of her gaze made me catch my breath, as if she too knew she only had a few moments to impart the truth to me. "Hannah, listen to me. Whatever you think you know about Simon. Whatever you think you may know, he's not what he seems." She took a deep breath and looked down at my hands before slowly withdrawing hers from them. "He saved me, Hannah. When anyone else would have just walked away and left me to rot in the system. He saved me. No matter what happens tonight, just remember that he has his reasons for everything he does."

"Why are you telling me this, Rue?" I looked down at her hands and then back to her honeyed eyes, searching them to try to understand what she was saying.

"Because I see the way he looks at you. And out of all the people I know in this world, Simon deserves some happiness. He's a fucking monster, yeah, but he's not your monster."

I heard the distinct click of the locking mechanism on my door and braced myself for the intense mixture of danger and sex appeal that was Simon Gallagher. But it was too late and my whispered, "Then who is?" died on the tip of my tongue as the door swung open with a bang and his dark scowl scanned every nook and cranny of the room as if he was looking for something before it settled over me. It took me just a moment to realize that he'd been scanning the room for threats. Threats against me.

My mouth went suddenly dry, and I wanted to melt into a pool of molten lava at his feet when his gaze dragged from the tips of my gold heels up and up and up. Caressing my thighs, brushing against the curve of my hips, lingering for half a second longer on the swell of my breasts against the deep V in the bodice of my dress, until finally, he met my eyes, and what I saw there made my breath catch and my heart stutter. I'd heard about that look, read about it in every romance novel, and wondered if it was real or just imagined words. *Starved* was the only way I could describe it. Simon Gallagher looked at me like he was a man starved and all I could think was how very much I wanted to be consumed by him.

CHAPTER TWENTY

SIMON

Hungry. It was the only word I could describe the way Hannah looked at me now. It took every ounce of control I had not to kick Rue out of the room and rip that goddammed gold dress off her body and make her come alive against its glittering sequins. I knew the moment the dress shop manager had shown it to me that it would be stunning on her. What I didn't know was that it would be a punch right to my very blue balls and kick into overdrive all the fantasies I'd been trying very hard to ignore over the past several days.

I watched the rise and fall of her breasts as she took in a few deep breaths, noticing how the gold cups of her dress pushed her cleavage up just like I'd imagined it. This desire, this hunger between us, was bordering on obsession. It was a dangerous game we were playing.

That I was playing. Because I knew without a doubt that if we were to go down that road to chaos, it would consume us both, and I didn't know if I'd be able to pull myself back from the edge this time.

Still, the dark part of my mind that desired to see her squirming beneath me, begging and pleading for something only I could give to her, couldn't let the opportunity pass without seeing her skin just a little flushed. It was as if someone else took control and spoke, "Look at you, princess. You clean up better than I thought." I intentionally let my eyes drag back down her body, noting how every inch of the dress hugged her delicious curves before bringing them back up. I'd thought that my comment would be met with her usual fire and disgust, but instead there was cool calculation with a hint of amusement there. She tossed her long hair over her shoulder, something I was glad to see that she'd kept down for the evening instead of pulling up in one of those typical intricate styles most women were fond of for these things.

"Why are you surprised, Si?" She moved towards me and it might have been my imagination, but I swore each step was exaggerated to make her hips sway in a sensual rhythm that I could barely take my eyes off of. I smelled the whisper of jasmine and vanilla before I noticed that her fingers were tracing lightly down the front lapel of my tuxedo. She'd mesmerized me so completely I hadn't realized how close she was standing to me now. Green eyes sparkled with a dark amusement as she tilted her head to the side and smirked. "You're my Fairy Godmother after all, aren't you? Although," her eyes widened in fake innocence, "... I don't seem to see your wings or your wand."

I couldn't help the smirk that spread across my lips as I pinned her hand to my chest. Her pulse fluttered wildly against the thumb I pressed lightly to her wrist and I knew that she wasn't as unaffected as she was trying to play off. I leaned down while pulling her in closer, not caring that Rue was watching us intently from her side of the room, and drew in a breath of the delicious scent that haunted my dreams now.

"Tsk, now now, princess, if you wanted to see my wand that badly, all you have to do is ask." I felt her stiffen at my crude remark and hid my grin in her hair as I carefully took the hand I'd pinned against my chest and began to drag it slowly down my chest towards the belt of my slacks. The wild beat of her pulse against my thumb never wavered and for a moment, I felt her fingers dip just a bit lower before she jerked her hand away and balled her fist up as if she was going to punch me right where I deserved. I grinned, noticing that the flush of her skin made the gold stand out even more. *Perfect.*

"Go take your wand and stick it up your ass, prick."

She turned her back to me and stomped back into the

room with a scowl. "You're right, he's not the Fairy Godmother, but he's absolutely a monster." She stopped in front of Rue and took a small gold clutch from her, opening it up and closing it with a huff. "And I still don't understand why you think I should be unarmed tonight. I'm not comfortable with this at all."

The look Rue gave her could only be described as apologetic and by the glare that she turned on me, I knew I'd be getting an earful later. It made me wonder what exactly had transpired between them in the last few days that would suddenly make them allies. I didn't want to think about the part of my brain that liked seeing the friendship that was forming between them.

"Because you're not the one with experience in these situations. You're more of a liability than anything right now." Her indignant snort had me raising a hand to interrupt the insults I knew she was getting ready to hurl my way. "A necessary liability, Hannah. A very calculated and important liability. But still one, just the same. Just stick to the plan and you won't even have a need for a weapon. I'll keep you safe."

"Riiiight." Her southern drawl spilled like warm honey from her lips as she turned to face me, eyes full of daggers. "Is that what you told my sister too? That you'd keep her safe? Because you did a pretty shitty job of it." Full lips curled in a snarl as she dragged her eyes from the tips of my shiny dress shoes up to my eyes, much in the same way I'd done to her. Gone was the hunger in her gaze I'd seen just a few moments earlier. It was like she'd pulled the pain of her grief and her suspicion of me and wrapped herself in the safety of its cocoon. I decided that I didn't like it and wanted the desire back in her eyes. Before I even realized what I was doing, or knew my mind was made up, I spoke.

"Rue, leave us."

Rue stiffened and began to gather up the makeup bags and toiletries. "Now Rue." I barked out, never taking my eyes off the seething golden goddess in front of me. Rue dropped everything and scurried out behind me, but not before I caught the worried glance towards Hannah and whispered, "Remember what I said." I let the comment slide, but made a mental note to find out exactly what the two of them had been discussing in my absence. When the door softly clicked shut, I stalked across the room towards her, loving how she stood her ground even when I came within mere inches of her.

God, she was beautiful in her anger. Tracing the outline of her jaw, I forced her head to tip back, so that she looked up at me. The gold in her dress brought out the same flecks of color in her eyes, making them sparkle. She didn't flinch or move at my touch, even when I traced her full bottom lip with my thumb.

"Why don't you tell me what's really bothering you,

lass?" Her nostrils flared, and the scent of jasmine and vanilla grew stronger in the air.

"I don't know what you're talking about." Her voice was low and husky when she replied. Did she even know that it had changed?

"Yes, you do. It's what you've been moping about since we left Atlanta. It's what's been weighing on your mind since that night at your sister's townhome. Say it." I wanted to groan as the pink tip of her tongue flicked out and wet her lips. My thumb continued to trace along her bottom lip and I growled out again, demanding. "Say what the fuck you've been thinking, Hannah."

She gasped, "Why? Why did you kiss me that night?"

I shook my head and murmured her name in warning, letting her know that I wasn't falling for her bullshit.

Her words tumbled out in a hurried whisper. "And why haven't you kissed me again?"

"Do you want me to kiss you again?" My hand drifted from her jaw, thumb pulling her lip downward with it before it stopped at the slender column of her throat, her pulse beating hard and fast against my palm, telling me the truth. She didn't speak, just shook her head no, and I almost laughed. "You're a terrible liar, lass."

"Don't call me la—"

I swooped the last few inches downward and captured her mouth in mine before she could finish her sentence. The taste of her exploded across my lips, and I finally released the pent-up groan. She was like honey and wine, dark and sweet all at the same time. Her mouth parted under mine and the little whimpers she let out drove me crazy. It was only half a step back towards the hotel bed and when the back of her knees hit the edge; she didn't hesitate to put her arms around my neck and cling to me as I followed her down.

"Simon..." the way she breathed my name had me nearly coming undone.

"You want to know why I kissed you, Hannah?" I growled against her lips. Her dress slid up her thigh as I traced its path, smooth skin burning hot under my palm. Higher and higher until I was tracing the lace of her panties, just barely sliding the tips of my fingers under the edge. Her hips arched upward, pressing her wet core into my palm. "Because from the moment you pinned me in that interrogation room, it was all I could think about. For the first time in a very long time, I felt alive. You awoke something in me, Hannah Kelly, and I don't know that I can ever go back."

CHAPTER TWENTY-ONE

Simon

Before she could say another word, I grazed my teeth along her earlobe, my fingers wandering further under the thin layer of her panties. "You can deny it all you want, princess, but you're soaked for me right now. You want me as badly as I want you."

Her hips pressed harder into me and she tilted her head back, eyes closed, "Si... please..."

"Please what Hannah?" My lips traced a slow path from her ear to the column of her throat then down further until the strap of her gown slipped from her shoulder and I could nuzzle the material aside to reveal the dark tip of her nipple. I blew a hot breath across it and watched in awe as it tightened for me, her back arching hard.

"Oh, for fucks sake Simon, stop teasing me." I

grinned as she grabbed fistfuls of my hair, pulling me towards her, and I sucked her nipple into my mouth. Groaning in satisfaction, she bucked into me. This was Hannah. Fiery, demanding. A woman who matched me pound for pound.

Continuing to lick and nibble on her full breast, I swept my fingers through her slickness, finding the nub there and grazing it with my thumb. Her pussy trembled as she squirmed beneath me. "Is this what you wanted, princess? My fingers, my cock, deep inside you?"

"God yes, please Si...."

My words triggered a reaction and at the same time that I felt a gush of her wetness flow around my fingers, I plunged two of them inside her hot core. Immediately, she clenched down in a tight grip that made my cock nearly explode in my trousers. "Fuck, you're so wet for me, baby. Such a good girl." I moved to her other breast, nearly ripping her dress off with my teeth to get to it before latching on and biting down on the nipple. She cried out and matched the rhythm of my fingers plunging in and out of her tightness.

"That's it, Hannah. Fuck my hand. Come for me, lass." She moaned and bucked against me as my thumb continued to press into her clit while I curved inward, finding and grazing over that sweet spot deep inside her. Over and over, my fingers hammered in her pussy. Her panting had me barely hanging on to the frayed edges of my control. I wanted nothing more than to rip the rest of her dress off her and feast on the delicious wetness that was soaking my hand at the moment. Palming her other breast, I reached for the peak of her nipple and gave it a hard pinch just as I growled around the nipple in my mouth. "Now Hannah, come for me. Now." She exploded, arching hard against me, her pussy fluttering in contractions around my fingers as she cried out in release.

I continued to lazily drag my fingers in and out of her, sliding them up and down her swollen folds and over the tip of her sensitive clit. She hissed and sighed as the aftershocks of her orgasm rode over her in waves. When she finally opened her eyes and looked at me, I withdrew my fingers and brought them to my mouth, tasting the delicious flavor that was uniquely Hannah. She watched with rapt attention as I licked every drop from them.

"Now, lass. Wasn't that better than one of your dime store romance novels?" Immediately her eyes flared with anger, but before she could retort, a hard knock sounded on the door followed by Evan's voice.

"Oi, Si! It's time to go."

I sat up, giving Hannah room to scramble away from me while she tried to fix the mess I'd made of her dress.

"You were decent. My vibrator does better. And we are not doing that again. It was an itch that needed to be scratched. That's all." She turned away from me towards the mirror on the wall, grabbing a tissue to dab at the smears of her makeup. "Dammit Simon, I need Rue, I can't fix this."

The knock sounded again, louder this time. "Simon? Hannah? Are you ready?"

"Give us a minute E- we will meet you downstairs." I called out before moving towards her and grabbing the tissue from her hand.

"Oh, I don't think so, lass. I think I fulfilled at least one of your dirty fantasies very, well." I wiped away the streaked makeup from her eyes, removing the excess liner and eyeshadow. I liked her better without it, anyway. Then leaned in until I pressed her back against the mirror, the flush from her orgasm still glistening on her skin.

"And we will absolutely do this again. Except next time, you'll be screaming your orgasm on my cock, not my fingers." Her gasp of shock and the way her pupils dilated told me all I needed to know about what my words did to her. Try as she might to deny it, Hannah Kelly was just as obsessed with me as I was with her.

With that, I turned around and made my way to the door, before calling out over my shoulder. "Be downstairs in five minutes, princess, and if you want a weapon, check your garment bag. I wasn't sure how much you'd resist. I'm glad to see I was right." And then I opened the door and stepped out into the hall where a frowning Evan was leaning against the wall waiting for me.

I didn't say a word, just turned and moved toward the elevators. Not that I had to say anything, but Evan spoke first.

"You're in over your head, Simon."

"I don't know what you're talking about."

The doors to the elevator swished open, and we stepped inside. Evan angrily jammed his finger into the button for them to close and turned toward me.

"You know exactly what the fuck I'm talking about, mate. This is Syria all over again."

I could still smell Hannah's scent clinging to me as I turned to look at the man who was my best friend and partner. The man who had been too literal hell and back with me. The one who had saved me from it as well. "Aye, you may be right, but *Hannah* is different. She's not Victoria."

"Oh yeah? Then when are you going to tell her the truth?"

My jaw clenched, my gut tightening. "When the time is right."

"And exactly when will that be, Simon, before or after she finds out what we've been doing this whole time?" He whirled in the tight space, his fists clenched at his side as he fought to regain control of his emotions. Not many saw this side of him. Not even Rue or Michael. They only knew him as the carefree playboy. Our enemies only knew him as a stone-cold killer. But I knew him better.

"We have a mission to complete, Evan." I kept my voice calm and cold, not letting the dark whisper of fear that tinged my thoughts come through. When Hannah knew the truth, would she run? Would she stay and listen? I already knew the truth though, even if I dared to hope against it. After tonight, I'd likely never see her again and all I'd have left of her is the memory of her taste on my lips.

"You gave her a weapon." It was a statement, not an accusation.

I nodded. "I did."

"Why?"

I sighed, "Because if we can't trust her, we can't trust anyone, Evan. She deserved to have a way to protect herself tonight."

He shook his head, and the elevator finally reached the lobby floor. "She's going to try to kill you, Simon. You know that, right?"

I nodded, reaching up to adjust my bowtie as the doors to the elevator opened up, and stepped outside. "Wrong Evan. She won't *try* to kill me. She will kill me."

And she would. As soon as Hannah knew how I'd tricked and betrayed her, she would absolutely turn on me. But not before my mission was complete. It was one last ride on the edge of chaos, only this time Hannah would be the one in control. Whether she drove us over the cliff or saved us all would be entirely up to her. All I could do was what I'd promised. I would finish the mission I'd failed all those years ago in Syria. Tonight, I would finally put the ghosts of my past to rest.

CHAPTER TWENTY-TWO

Hannah

For a bunch of nerds and reclusive scientists, they sure knew how to throw a party. The event space that only a few hours ago had been filled with lectures and presentations was now transformed into a glittering ball space fit for a high society swaray. Men and women more accustomed to lab coats and beakers moved around the room in stiff tuxedos and ball gowns holding champaign glasses. Low conversations and laughter swirled around the ballroom and I noted how more relaxed most of the attendees were. Clearly, they had put aside their stuffy academia for the night and decided to enjoy themselves.

After Simon had left me alone in my hotel room, I stayed pressed against the mirror, staring at the bed where he'd made me come undone with just a few dirty words and skilled fingers. The memory of his gravelly voice coaxing and demanding my release had me trembling all over again. My thoughts swirled. Since learning about the secret life my sister had been living, I'd been lost and confused. But for the first time since I'd gotten the call about her murder, I felt like I was thinking clearly again.

Was Simon Gallagher an arrogant, dangerous, and murderous mercenary? Yes, absolutely. But somehow none of that bothered me and I finally realized why. My job meant I'd come across the worst of the worst in the dangerous criminal category. The kind that would make your skin crawl and leave you checking over your shoulder for weeks to come. Simon wasn't like them. He didn't make me feel like I'd walked through a spiderweb of pure evil. In fact, if I was being completely honest with myself, Simon was the first man that I felt like I didn't have to hide myself from. He saw me, the real me, and he didn't run in fear that I might have bigger balls than him. If anything, he pushed me to be my true self.

Which is why, when he'd demanded the truth out of me, I'd given it. I couldn't deny it anymore. I wanted Simon like I'd never wanted any other man before. The only thing that had been holding me back from giving in had been the idea that somehow I was betraying Sybil's memory by being with him. But I no longer thought that Simon was responsible for her death, at least not directly. Whatever Sybil had been involved in, I couldn't even be sure that it was what had killed her in the first place. The investigation hadn't even had a chance to take place, and once I was done here, it would become my top priority.

A waiter in a crisp-looking uniform floated by me and I reached out to snag a glass of champaign from his tray, tipping it back and downing the contents in one gulp. If I'd surprised him, he was too professional to make a face and merely took my empty glass, smoothly replacing it with a full one, and then swirled away to disappear into the crowd.

I was standing in a small alcove created by two giant ferns topping decorative pillars. Simon had left briefly to do a reconnaissance of the room and had instructed me to wait for him here. That had been roughly fifteen minutes ago by my count and the number of times a waiter or waitress had passed by my little hiding spot. Tapping an impatient foot, I sipped the second glass of champagne more slowly.

The intel Simon and his band of misfits had shared with me said that the broker between the Abromov group and a third-party arms dealer would be going down tonight. Presumably, that broker was supposed to be meeting with Sybil, aka me, before this happened to exchange information. He would be passing on files that contained a complete list of weapons caches and their locations, in addition to the source of their funding. Once we had this file, we could finally expose the Abromov group for what they were and cut the head off of at least one evil snake in the world. Not to mention potentially getting weapons that would kill hundreds of innocent civilians out of the hands of warlords and terrorists.

After watching another waiter do their twirl and swirl around the main ballroom, I tossed the rest of my champagne into the fern next to me and began to move towards the food tables on the opposite side of the room. I was tired of just being stuck on the sidelines until I was called on. I wanted to *do* something and with the thigh holster and compact Ruger pistol Simon had neatly tucked away for me inside the garment bag; I felt more confident.

Doing my best to keep my face under an emotionless mask that I thought would resemble the look that Sybil would wear, I wove around mingling people, my eyes scanning the crowd for anyone that might stand out. Conversations flowed around me and just as I was about to turn and do another pass toward the outside edge of the ballroom floor, I felt a rough hand grab my arm. Turning in surprise, I had to swallow the fear that threatened to overwhelm me when I saw who it was.

Sergei Abromov towered above me, his silver hair cut close to his square head, and ice-blue eyes cut through me like a knife. He looked mostly like the pictures I'd seen of him with Sybil if but a little older. Still, a handsome man, still intimidating in his posture and size. And by the way, he glared down at me and from the tight grip he kept on my arm; he was furious.

"What are you doing here, dorogáya? It is very dangerous for you to be seen right now."

I gulped, not knowing what to say. On the one hand, Sergei thought I was Sybil, which meant that our ruse had worked and I looked enough like her that even he couldn't tell the difference. On the other hand, he was never supposed to be here and now I had to figure out a way to get away from him to alert the others.

Carefully and with what I hoped was enough of the haughtiness in my tone that had made everyone around Sybil feel as if they were talking to royalty, I glanced down at where he gripped my arm and then fixed him with a stony glare. "Sergei, I'm sure there is a more *private* area we can go to have this discussion, is there not?"

At the same moment, the earpiece, carefully hidden by the thick waves of my hair, crackled to life. "Cinderella, where are you?" Simon's dark voice came over the line and I felt a surge of relief. Sergei cocked one thick brow at me but released the grip he'd kept on my arm. "Da, of course, moya lyubov', forgive me. It merely startled me to see you in public after we'd discussed the risks."

"Cinderella, answer me, now." Simon's voice growled insistently through the mic.

"Well, Sergei Abromov, how could I fear risks when I have such a *fairy godmother* like you always looking out for me?" God, I hoped the high-tech mics Rue had rigged us with were doing their job and transmitting this to the team. They needed to know the danger we were in. If Sergei got even a whiff of suspicion about who I really was, the entire mission was blown.

"Hannah, do *not let* him take you anywhere. Get away from him. I'm coming."

Sergei stared at me for half a second and then barked out a deep baritone laugh. "Ahh, you are continuously surprising me, my darling. Come, let us get you away from these nizkiy uroven', people, before they rub off on you and you truly turn into a tykva." He took my elbow and began to guide me through the crowd towards the edge of the room and a set of double doors that led to lecture rooms and halls.

"A tykva?" I asked as I scanned the room, desperately hoping to see a dark head towering above the throng of people and heading in my direction.

"Da, a pumpkin." He leaned down closer to my ear with a leering grin and whispered, "Although I do like the idea of seeing you play the helpless princess, but I'm afraid I am no Prince Charming." A sick shudder went through me as a whisper of a thought formed.

"No? Well, if you aren't the prince, then who are you exactly?" I slowed my steps, attempting to stall and get his reply. The earpiece crackled again. "I'm almost there, Hannah. Get away from him and head towards the buffet tables. Evan will intercept."

Sergei paused and drew himself up to his full height, his face suddenly as cold and imperious as a statue. "You know who I am. I am Šimon Sergei Abromov and I am your king." And then he was leaning down again, his leer turning even darker and twisted as his grip on my elbow turned painful. "And you disobeyed your king tonight, my little *Zolushka*, Cinderella, do not think you will escape your punishment."

I grunted as he jerked my arm painfully and practically dragged me the remaining few feet towards the doors. Panic set in and I began to struggle. "Sergei, I don't know what you think you're doing, but I am not going in there with you."

"Oh, I know exactly what I'm doing. You have gone too long unchecked dorogáya. I let you handle the nasty business with our weapons buyers and didn't question your sick fascination with your sister, but this is outright disobedience. I will not tolerate it."

I dug my heels in and threw my weight back just as we reached the doors. "What do you mean, my sick fascination with my sister?"

But Sergei didn't pause or seem to care that I was

resisting his pull on my arm. He merely pushed through the doors and hauled me forward with him. I had no choice but to follow or fall flat on my face. When the doors closed behind us he stop and turned back to me, his snarling face coming a mere inch from mine. I tried not to flinch as his hot breath brushed over me. Where the fuck was Simon?

"You are seconds away from earning your punishment now, Sybil. Do not test me on this. Now, our buyer is here. The deal is done, but he is eager to meet you. You will speak with him and then you will go back to your room. Do you understand? This is your final warning." And with that, he pushed me away from him, causing me to stumble, and then took a few steps back, casually adjusting his tuxedo jacket as he did so. Just as I was catching my breath and reeling from the shock of his words, what did he mean by "sick fascination with your sister?" He turned and looked over his shoulder.

"Ah, Mr. Callahan. I hope we did not keep you waiting." And there, in the dim lighting, a tall figure emerged that I immediately recognized. *Simon.* Confusion flooded through me.

Sergei continued, "I was just telling Dr. Kelly how eager you were to meet her."

Simon slid those dark grey eyes towards me, a cold mask of indifference in his gaze. "Yes. After our conversation on the phone a few weeks ago, I decided I must meet the brilliant scientist who designed these new guidance systems herself. I'm keen to test them out and I'm sure my clients will appreciate all the effort that went into brokering them for us."

Sergei chuckled and moved forward to clasp Simon on the shoulder like they were old comrades. Meanwhile, Simon's eyes never left mine, conveying something I couldn't see beyond the overwhelming clarity that was forming. Simon, Šimon, the phone call, the voice, the nerdy aristocratic scientist that Sybil was disappearing for days on end with. It wasn't Simon, at least not *this* Simon. It was *Sergei*. Simon Gallagher had never worked with my sister. She'd never been a spy, working undercover like he'd told me. She had been his target the entire time.

The world around me turned into a red haze of fury. He'd lied to me. From the beginning, it had all been a lie. And he'd used me. All of them had. Before I knew what I was doing, the Ruger was in my hand and I was pointing it, not at Sergei, but Simon.

CHAPTER TWENTY-THREE

Hannah

"Where is my sister?"

Sergei turned around in shock, but Simon's gaze never faltered. He looked at me with what I could only describe as a quiet resignation. He knew the fucking bastard had known that it would come to this.

"Moya lyubov'! What are you doing? Put the gun away, Mr. Callahan is our friend." Sergei started towards me until I flicked the gun in his direction.

"Shut up, *Šimon.*" I drew the pronunciation out like it would be pronounced in Russian, Sem-yon. Clever, my sister, to pronounce his name the English way and not make it obvious that the man she was dating was Russian. "You have no idea who this man is, and trust me when I say he is *nothing* to me." Sergei stopped, confusion lining his face as he looked from Simon and then back to me.

"Where the fuck is my sister?" I growled at Simon again. "Did you kill her?"

"I didn't kill your sister."

I snorted, my gun trained on him once again. "Then where the fuck is she, Si? Why did you drag me halfway across the world on some god damned goose chase of a mission, knowing that she was alive?"

"Why, to get me to come out of hiding, of course."

All three heads whipped towards the voice that suddenly appeared out of thin air, like a ghost. A ghost that brought me immediate joy and despair. Of the three of us, I wasn't sure who looked more shocked, myself or Sergei. Simon, however, didn't even blink, just stared with a stoney expression in place.

"Sissy?" My voice choked back a sob as I took in the sight of my beautiful little sister, alive, breathing, and in the same room as me once again. Only she didn't look as thrilled to see me as I was to see her. She stood a few feet away with her hands tucked into crisp grey slacks that were topped by a white linen shirt, hair pulled into a loose bun at the base of her neck. Everything about her was cool elegance and sophistication, still. But the look on her face was the same look she would make when she'd had to take out the garbage or do a chore as a little girl. Like it was all beneath her.

"I told you to trust me and here you are ruining everything again."

I opened my mouth to reply with "What do you..." and then realized she wasn't even looking at me, but at Sergei. He spread his hands and shook his head in confusion. "My love, I am so sorry." He looked back at me and curled his lips in disgust. "I see now why you hated her so much. She is just a poor imitation."

She removed a hand from her pocket and inspected the cuticles of one delicately manicured nail. "And to think you thought *she* could have possibly been me. I am truly insulted, *Šimon.*"

I shook my head, trying to clear the confusion and overwhelming emotions that were threatening to drop me to the floor. "Sissy, what the fuck is going on? Why are you here?"

Sybil stepped further into the room, moving towards Sergei, delicately cupping the side of his face as she stared up at him. "Oh Hannah, if only you could understand what you do for the people that you love. The depths that you will go to. The things that you will submit yourself to. Although, every time you thought you might get to experience that, you were left-abandoned. Alone. Used." She leaned upward and placed a soft kiss on his lips before turning back to me. "But then it looks like you're experiencing that all over again, aren't you?" Her smile was smug and satisfied as she looked at Simon and me. Simon never said a word, just stood there watching her. A predator watching his prey.

When she didn't get the reaction she was looking for from him, she turned back to me and crossed her arms over her chest in annoyance. "But then you never knew when to back off, didn't you? Always whining to Mom and Dad. Always *there*. But you finally stopped and learned your place. Did you get my little reminder? I thought that would keep you from following me, but I guess you forgot the lesson." Her voice was dripping with disgust and hatred. I stared at my sister like I was seeing her for the first time. The Sybil that was in front of me was not the sister I'd grown up with, wasn't she?

The memory of finding the paper bag and haunting polaroid resurfaced.

"That was you? You left that picture for me?"

"Good job Hannah. You finally got something right."

I shook my head, refusing to acknowledge what was in front of me. "Sybil, I have no idea what is happening right now or why you're here. But you were *dead*. Mom and dad think you've been murdered. Why would you do that to them? To me?" The tears were falling now, hurt and anger making my voice shake. "Sissy, why?"

"Oh please, our parents never cared about me. It was always about *you*. Hannah this and Hannah that. They never stopped talking or bragging about you." Her beautiful face fell, contorting into a thing of mottled and ugly rage. "It should have been *me. Just me.*"

She advanced toward me, one slow step at a time, the

curl of her lips and the snarl of her voice sending cold shivers down my spine. "I couldn't understand it. I was the smart one. I was the pretty one. They should have loved me the most. But no, you were always there. Always in the way. They didn't believe me that you weren't supposed to be there. That it was supposed to be just me. So I had to convince you instead. I had to make you understand what I wanted was the most important and best thing for you. For us."

The horror dawned as I watched her take on a crazed expression. "The promise."

Her teeth glinted as she snapped a sadistic smile. "The promise. Don't you remember Hans?"

I shook my head, my breaths becoming fast and shallow as I was transported back into a memory. "You were mad we couldn't go to the pageant in Macon. The Cherry Tree festival." Sybil just nodded, the crazy grin still in place on her lips. "Because I'd just gotten a new puppy..." Oh god, I remembered. I remembered now.

"You killed Daisy. You threw her over the fence to the neighbor's dogs and they mauled her to death." My voice sounded hollow, as if I was speaking from a distance, an objective observer of the scene that was being replayed in my memory. "And you told me you'd do that to everything I loved if I ever got in your way again."

Sybil's smile grew wider, and she clapped her hands in delight. "Good girl Hannah! Do you remember what was in the paper bag?" She looked over at Sergei, who was calmly watching the entire exchange with a bemused expression. "Do you see, darling? I've always had a creative flair for these things. Go on, Hannah, tell Sergei what was in the bag."

I felt like I was going to be sick. Once the blocks on memories came down, so many little things came back to me. The heads of my dolls were torn off and left for me to find around my room. Her standing over me in the middle of the night as I slept, a kitchen knife in her hand, then giggling and running away. The brakes on my bike cut so that when I tried to stop or slow down on the hill near our house, I couldn't. I'd nearly broken my neck when I'd finally been flung over the handlebars after hitting a rock. And always it was before she would ask mom and dad for something, usually a pageant show or science competition.

But the paper bag was by far the worst. After that day, I'd never objected to anything she wanted to do. I'd become Sybil's number one fan and supporter. Everything I had was hers. It was the afternoon that she'd thrown Daisy over the fence. Our parents weren't home yet, but I was fully planning on telling them what she'd done. All the other little things I'd let go, just thinking she was being a brat. But this was too far. They had to know. They had to *believe me*.

"It was Daisy." I croaked out and looked at Simon,

not wanting to see the look of sick delight that lit up Sybil's eyes. She clung to every word I spoke, like an addict who was getting her fix. And I realized in a way she was, my anguish, my pain, were her drug of choice. Simon's grey eyes met mine with sympathetic understanding. He'd been there when I'd pulled out the polaroid from that paper bag. "On the picture that night, in the bag all those years ago, it was Daisy. I remember now." Each word came easier and before I knew it, the whole story began to stumble, word after word, out of my mouth. Like the floodgates were opened and I couldn't stop.

"She'd gone over to the house after Mr. Bulloch's dogs had finally finished *toying* with her." Bile rose in my throat, but I fought it back. "And she'd brought it to me like it was a present. I couldn't stop screaming." I turned towards my sister, sickened by the memories that were replaying like a movie over and over in my head. "And you just laughed. I guess you wanted to make sure I understood what would happen if I broke that promise again."

Sybil closed her eyes with a sigh. "Mmmm... such a hard, difficult lesson that had to be learned that day. But you did so good for such a long time, Hannah! I never had to ask mommy or daddy for anything again. You were almost the *perfect* sister, even if you never would just go away like I wanted you to."

"So you faked your death to get away from your annoying sister? To what? Run away with your demented boyfriend and sell weapons to terrorists? How is this in any way better than the life you had?"

"Actually, no, I had no intention of doing anything of the sort, but then your little spy boyfriend had to stick his nose where it didn't belong."

I frowned. "He's not my boyfriend. What do you mean?"

She smirked and then turned her back to me, speaking over her shoulder as she walked away, Sergei following closely behind. "It doesn't matter, Hannah. I'm still going to get what I want. Your time is almost up and once I explain to Mommy and Daddy about the tragedy of your life, they will understand. How you couldn't cope with your professional life falling apart and how you were always jealous of my success. How you captured me and staged the whole thing. Well, let's just say it really will be like Hannah Kelly doesn't exist anymore."

A sick feeling took root in my stomach and I marched after her, determined to stop her from leaving. "Sybil, this is madness. I was never jealous of you. I *love* you."

But she wasn't listening and suddenly I was being flung to the ground as a loud explosion rocked the building. Glass and cement rained down around us as smoke filled the room. I could hear screams coming from the ballroom on the other side of the wall. My ears were ringing as I coughed and felt a small smatter of blood drip down my face.

As I groaned and tried to get to my feet, I felt powerful hands pull at me and looked up at Simon, who was now covered in the dust of debris. I couldn't hear what he was saying. The entire world seemed like it was encased in cotton. I felt nauseated and sick as I tried to shake my head no, eyes darting around for Sybil. Where had she gone?

Suddenly, with a loud pop, Simon's voice came in crystal clear. "Hannah, we have to go. Come on."

"No, not without Sybil."

"She's gone Hannah, she left as soon you hit the ground. This was a coordinated attack, which means the clean-up crew will be on their way in to make sure we're down for good." He pulled at me just as a bullet whizzed by my ear. I turned to see men in black masks and uniforms pour through a set of double doors on the opposite side of the room. The room spun harder, and I stumbled, trying to keep up with him.

"Si, stop." But he didn't listen, just pushed through the doors and made for the back exit of the ballroom, where we'd originally planned our escape from.

Once on the street, I could hear the wail of sirens in the distance and we were swept up into the throng of people who were running from the building along with us. There was no time to think or get him to pause in the push from the crowd. When we rounded the corner in the opposite direction of where the crowd was running, I recognized the black van Michael was waiting for us at the end of the block. The sliding door was flung open just as gunfire rang out against the cobblestone and Simon pushed me forward before slamming it closed behind me.

"Simon, no!" I tried to open it again to stop him, but it was too late. The van was peeling away and Simon had disappeared into the shadows just as two uniformed men came barreling towards us.

"Michael stop, we have to go back for him."

"No can do doll. Simon's orders were that if anything went tits-up, we got you tits out."

I turned to look out the back of the van, holding on to the edge of my seat as Michael once again took a hairpin turn around another corner. I couldn't see anything but the glow of a fire burning against the brick and stone of the institute as it grew smaller in the distance. Simon had used me, lied to me, and still, the whisper of worry settled like a stone in a gut. *Pathetic.* The dark voice that lingered like an ever-present passenger in the back of my mind resurfaced. Only this time, I recognized it for what it was. Sybil's voice.

I shook the thought away and turned around. Maybe I was pathetic. But I knew what I wasn't, and that was a fool. Simon Gallagher had played me like a harp string. But no more. I was done playing by everybody else's rules in a game I had no chance of winning. Sybil's game, Simon's game, the Hildago syndicate, and whoever had set me up. They were about to learn that when I made a promise; I kept it. And I had promised to make them all pay.

I looked up to see Michael's black gaze watching me from the rearview mirror, and a wicked smile curved my lips upward. He frowned and looked like he was about to comment, but then I turned away. I was done talking to these people. They thought they were the monsters? Good. I hunted monsters.

CHAPTER TWENTY-FOUR

Hannah

One week later...

"Mon cher, I know you don't want to talk to me, but please, you have to at least hear me out." Rue's voice on the other end of the line was pleading with me.

"Wrong Rue, I don't have to do shit with you, to you, or for you. I told you when we landed last week. I'm done with all of your and especially Simon's bullshit." I brought two fingers to the bridge of my nose and pinched it in frustration. I don't know why I'd decided to take her call but after a week of constant texts and phone calls from everyone in the group other than Simon, I'd decided that out of all of them, Rue was the one I could tolerate the most.

"Hannah, I'm sorry. None of us wanted to bring you

into this, least of all Simon, but it was the only way we could get to Abromov."

"Fuck you, Rue. You're lying again. Do you mean my sister? It was the only way you could get to my sister, and you used me to do it."

I whirled and kicked a wayward takeout container that had spilled off my coffee table. It was littered with containers and articles, newspapers, and printed papers, all containing snippets of information on the Abromov group. There were also a few from the Hildago syndicate thrown in there, but it hadn't been my main focus. Mainly just a distraction when I felt I hit a brick wall tracking down Sybil. And those brick walls happened a lot.

A deep sigh came from the line. "Look, I know you have no reason to believe me or trust me. But we need your help."

"Hah! That's rich. Simon sending you to do his dirty work because he's too afraid to ask me himself? Well, guess what? The answer is still the same. Fuck you."

"Simon is missing." Rue's voice was low and strained. The worry was clear, even though she remained calm.

"And? He probably crawled back into whatever god-forsaken hole he came out of. Why are you telling me this?"

"Because we think Sybil has him."

I stopped dead in my tracks, my eyes coming to the

picture of me and Sybil from when we were kids. The same picture that Simon had picked up and scrutinized just a few short weeks ago. "You're lying. You just want me to help you find Sybil again and you're using Simon as the glass slipper this time. Well, I'm done being made an ass of by your little team of fucked up rats, Rue."

"This isn't a fucking game, Hannah." Rue's voice shook now. "He is really missing. We've tried everything to locate him, but he's gone completely black on comms. And honestly, we don't even know if Sybil really has him. It's just the best lead we have and out of anyone, you're the best qualified to find her."

I ground my teeth, rage seeping from every pore in my body. How dare they do this to me? How dare *Simon* do this to me? I didn't want to get dragged back into their game of lies and half-truths. Of learning to care for someone, only to realize they fed you a lie. Mostly, I was angry they were using my sister as an excuse to drag me back into their twisted games.

"I don't care if Sybil has him or the fucking leader of the Islamic caliphate. I. Am. Done. The answer is no, so stop calling me. Stop texting me. Go play your spy games and leave me out of it." I was just about to hit end on the call when Rue's voice came crackling over the line one last time.

"Fine. Fine. This will be goodbye for good, my friend. But there is one last thing: something Simon promised me to deliver to you. It should be outside your door now. I'm sorry, Hannah, for all of it. I truly am." And then the line went dead, and I was left staring at the screen of my phone. I should have felt some sort of elation at telling her exactly how I felt and thought, but instead, all I could feel was hollowness. I put my phone down on the table full of clutter and looked at my door, wondering what she could have meant and if it was a gift or a threat.

Curiosity got the better of me and when I opened the door, I found a brown manilla envelope with my name and address written on it. No return sender. Picking it up, I carried it back inside and decided that my brief idea that it might be a bomb was unwarranted. Dumping the contents out on my table, I frowned when I saw a USB thumb drive and a note written on plain white card stock.

"I keep my promises. - S,"

Dropping the note, I picked up the USB drive and sat down on my couch as I reached for my laptop. Then I plugged in the drive and waited for whatever was on it to pop up.

A video player opened and for a moment I was confused as the screen was just black, but then I suddenly realized what I was looking at. It was the CCTV footage from the evidence locker. He'd remembered. The excitement built as I fast-forwarded through the hours of footage until I found the date and time that the evidence had been stolen. Simon may have put me through absolute hell, but at least he'd done this for me.

Gotcha! I watched with a rising giddiness as I saw a dark figure come into the frame. My hand was reaching excitedly for my phone to text David. I watched as a slender hand picked up the pen from the clipboard that the security officers on duty handed over and sign my name in a perfect, almost flawless imitation of my handwriting. And then I watched as what looked like a copy of my badge was scanned and the officer pressed a button to open up the gate that would let me into the back rooms where the evidence was stored. I paused the video before the person could disappear from the frame.

"Come on! Where is your face? Show me your face, bitch, so I can find you and kick your ass." I muttered in frustration. The film was so grainy and dark that nothing stood out to me. It figured that the greatest law enforcement agency in the world would have the absolute shittiest security cameras. I cursed a few more times and then zoomed in, trying to make out any details I could.

My blood ran cold when I found it. Behind the security desk in the upper corner of the little office where the attendant sat was an old-fashioned disk mirror. The kind people were more used to seeing in shopping malls to catch thieves. It was what was reflected in the mirror, though, that made my heart beat like it was going to explode and the sweat drip from my brow. My thumb pressed down on the FaceTime button on my phone and I placed it down next to my computer, waiting. A breathy voice answered, "Hannah?"

I didn't answer for a few moments, just stared at the screen as silent tears dripped down my face. "Hannah, what's wrong?"

Finally, clearing my throat, I picked up the phone and turned the screen around to face my computer and the zoomed-in frame. "Mon Dieu. Hannah, is that who I think it is?"

"It is. And I'm in."

"Wait... so you'll help us? You'll help find Simon?" Rue's voice held anxious excitement.

"No. I'm going to help you find my sister. And then you're going to help me bring her to justice."

Rue was silent for a few heartbeats before she breathed, "Ok Hannah. Ok, we will do it your way this time mon cher."

"Yeah, you will." And then I hung up and stared at the image of the woman in the mirror who stared mockingly back at me. The image that in almost every sense was me. But it wasn't and as I fingered the St. Michaels pendant that hung between my breasts, I felt the numbness give away to ice-cold rage. "I'm coming for you, sister dear, and I'm not afraid anymore." I knew it was just my imagination, but it looked like the mirror image of Sybil's face twisted into an evil grin back in response.

A NOTE FROM THE AUTHOR

Hello, lovelies! Thank you so much for reading my book. I genuinely hope you enjoy the story I've told and any future stories to come. As a self-published author I 100% rely on your support to continue writing. What's the best way to do that? Leave a review and share the book with others! Even a simple star rating, good or bad, helps us authors reach more readers and become better at our craft. That being said, if you come across any errors, grammatical or otherwise in the book, please let me know as soon as possible before you give that star rating! I welcome all helpful feedback.

I look forward to hearing from you!- Anne
authoranneroman@gmail.com
www.anneromanauthor.com

ACKNOWLEDGMENTS

I will probably never write an acknowledgment this long again, but I couldn't end my first book without saying thank you to some very important people. First, my husband. Z- thank you for supporting me, loving me, and most importantly, not complaining when you had to fall asleep to the sound of me typing away late at night. I love you!

Secondly, Debbie. Thank you for being my teacher, the voice of wisdom and encourager when I wanted to give up. Your experience and guidance (not to mention all the books on writing!) were invaluable. I will forever be grateful for you and your friendship. You're stuck with me now!

Third, to my Book Tour Gals. What a rollercoaster this year has been! But through it all, the steady support of your friendship has seen me through some really hard times as well as some amazing times. I'm so very thankful for all of you and count you as some of my closest friends.

And lastly, to my Aunts. Aunt Rae & Sonya, this book is for you. You taught me to love reading, love writing, and most importantly how to be a strong and independent woman. "Duncan women can do anything!" This strength and fierceness is something that I hope to bring to life in my characters. So much of me is because of what you both poured into me and I am so thankful for it. I love you so much. xoxo- Anne

ABOUT THE AUTHOR

Anne Roman is an emerging author of dangerously addictive romance novels. When not writing you can find Anne playing uber driver for her family, ingesting way too much caffeine in the form of coffee or energy drinks, and genuinely enjoying life. She lives with her husband, four children, two cats, and one dog in a small rural community in Georgia.

PREVIEW

CHAPTER ONE

"Honey badger come, come in honey badger." The radio tucked into my low-visibility armor kit crackled to life. I ignored it, just like I ignored the tingling itch of sweat dripping down the back of my neck into the moisture-soaked keffiyeh. The neck scarf was supposed to protect me from the dust and dirt that seemed to coat everything in this god-forsaken country, but on days like today, when the sun beat down on us in waves, all it did was add another layer of irritation to erode my already shitty mood.

I'd been tucked into the side of a mountain in the southern mountain ranges of Syria for going on two days and would be there for several more if necessary. It all depended on when and if the intel U.S. forces had shared with us was accurate. And they typically were. The radio crackled to life again. "Honey badger, please respond."

There was a movement of rock next to me, a shift so subtle not many would have noticed it. But I was trained to know when my partner moved even a minuscule inch, and they had the same training.

"You better answer him." My eyes slid toward the blur of brown and gray that blended seamlessly into the mountain terrain next to me. To anyone who stood even a few inches away from our location, it would have appeared as if the rocks themselves were talking.

"I'm not fecking answering. He can use my damn call sign."

"He's just going to keep on until you respond."

At that, the radio crackled to life again. "Honey-" I snatched it from my kit and hit the transmitter.

"Call me fecking honey badger one more time E and I swear on my mother I'll cut your balls off and feed them to one."

There was a slight pause before a voice came across the radio again, only it wasn't Evan. "Reaper cut the shit. This is Colonel Smith. Have you seen any movement?"

A soft chuckle came from the rock pile next to me and I cut a glare toward it, clearing my throat. "Apologies sir, that's a negative. No movement on the southern ridge."

"Fine. Get to the extraction point. We need your team elsewhere."

I felt the tick of the muscles in my jaw as I clenched it and took a few seconds to pause before I answered. "Sir, I do think you should reconsider. We're already fully in place and ready to engage. The intel we received from the Americans said that this is the most likely route the target's men will be taking."

The same sharp voice came across the radio once more. "Your concerns are duly noted. However, we have other more pressing matters that need your expertise. Pack it up and get to the extraction point."

"Rodger, Sir. Reaper out."

I barely heard the whisper of movement before I felt the light hand on my shoulder and glanced up at my partner. Her face was covered with brown and gray camouflage paint but I could make out the sparkle of blue eyes that smiled down at me.

I stood, removing the rocks and pieces of brittle shrub that helped me blend in with my environment

"What's so funny?"

There was a flash of white as she grinned and then turned away beginning to pack up her gear and disassemble the high-powered rifle that would have left the brains of anyone within 500 yards a mere stain in the dirt.

"Oh, just thinking about our days in selection. Remember how we thought we were going to save the world?"

I snorted, beginning to help her pack up the gear, before slinging the heavy ruck over my shoulders. After eight years of crossing mountainous terrain, icy slopes, and arid desserts, the weight of the pack felt familiar and comfortable. "I remember trying to get you to kiss me outside the slop tent when it was our turn on KP duty."

It was her turn to snort as she slung her pack over her shoulders and I let her take the lead as we made our way down the mountainside. "Hmm...and do you need another reminder of what happened to you then?"

I grinned, "Tsk, come now my little trigger-happy tease, you wouldn't want to hurt your favorite part of me."

"You don't need your tongue for me to use my favorite part of you Simon Gallagher."

We rounded the low cropping of boulders just as the wind around us began to pick up and the dove gray Osprey landed a few hundred yards from us in the hard-packed dirt.

"Oh, well now, looks like I'm going to have to do my best to make my tongue your other favorite part of me." I grinned as she threw me an eye roll and then sprinted out from behind the boulders towards the waiting Osprey. I could just barely make out the words over the wind whipping around us from the whirling blades. "You'll have to catch me first!"

Simon

The cold slap of water on my face cut through the hazy fog of my dreams and I woke up with a start. It took only seconds for reality to set in. A quick check of my extremities told me I was in the same position I'd been in for the last several days, strapped to a cold exam table with just a thin sheet covering my lower half. At least they left the sheet this time.

I swallowed past the dry ache in my throat, reminding me that I couldn't remember the last time I'd had anything to drink.

I tried to open my swollen eyes and turn towards where I thought the water had come from but could only make out rough shapes. Shape one was large and hovered off to the side. Shape two was smaller and came closer as my head tried to angle toward it. Cold hands traced across my chest toward my ribs and I winced when they lingered over the bruises there. From the way the pain radiated sharply with every breath I inhaled, I was pretty sure a couple of them were broken.

"Did you love her?"

The soft voice pierced my ears and I knew who was touching me now. Bile rose in my throat and it took all the willpower I had not to visibly recoil at the feel of her hand tracing languid patterns over my bruises. I knew better than to stay silent however, it would only give her reason to continue to touch me.

"I don't know what you're talking about."

Her tongue clicked in soft disapproval. "Oh come now, Simon. You were moaning her name just now in your sleep. I wonder, does my sister know about your other lover? About our history?"

I winced as sharp nails gripped the tender edge of one of my ribs, curling around it and digging in with slow and steady pressure.

"You know I loved her." I barked the words out with a hiss of pain, sweat pooling at my temples. I worried that those fingers would continue to dig into me but my answer seemed to surprise her and she pulled her hand away.

"*Did I?*" The slow, languid, petting began again. Her hand traced all the patterns of my beaten and bruised body.

"Ayou, you knew. And she loved me until you poisoned her mind." I waited for the overwhelming sense of grief and rage to come whenever I spoke about Victoria, but it didn't. Instead, there was just a dull ache at the memory of the dream I'd been lost in.

"I think we remember things very differently." Fingernails trailed over open cuts on my skin and I hissed again at the sensation. The mix of soft caresses, almost sensual in the way she skimmed her fingers over my broken body, and the pain she inflicted at the same time, made me nauseated. "How did she die?"

The question was asked innocently enough, but I knew it was anything but. She leaned towards me, her eyes dilated and shining with intense interest, even though she maintained an emotionless expression.

"You should know. You killed her." The pain made my accent, so carefully cultivated to be hidden over the years so that I could blend in with the environment around me, spill across my busted lips in a rough brogue.

"Simon, poor Simon, all these years spent hunting me. Looking for revenge." A disappointed pout turned her full lips down and for a moment I thought of another pair of pouty lips. "And yet you're still blaming someone else for your own mistakes. I wasn't the one who put the bullet in Tory's head."

"Oh, you did. You set up the meeting. And you manipulated Tory into helping you. You might not have pulled the trigger, but you loaded the damn gun."

"Hmm...." Was the only sound she made as she continued her inspection of every cut and bruise on my body.

I continued, ignoring the sickening sensation that traveled up my thighs to my gut as her nails dug into another deep gash. "I should have known. The way she talked about you." Emotions threatened to overwhelm me but I'd be dammed if I let the evil bitch see it.

After the Colonel had pulled us back from our over-watch position we'd learned that new intel had suggested that the leader of a local extremist sect had been tasked as the middleman to broker a deal between a new arms dealer and the caliphate. The chatter on some of the channels indicated the dealer had come into possession of some new drone technology from the United States. How they'd managed to get their hands on billions of dollars worth of tech like that blew my mind and part of me thought it was just a hoax. A distraction from the terrorist training camps they were building up in other areas.

When I'd grumbled to Tory about my lack of faith in our leadership she'd just glared at me, her lips pressed together in a thin line of resentment. I knew that look. It was the look that came right before the "*I told you so.*"

It was an old argument between us. For the past couple of years, Victoria had grown more and more disgruntled with our line of work. And not just our work, but the tedious toll that constant missions took on us. More than once she'd mentioned that our necks were on the line for people who only ever sat behind a teleprompter and used our services to elevate their own positions. The conversation always made me uncomfortable. While we weren't sitting on stacks of cash, being off the record of any military unit in Her Majesty's service meant that we were paid handsomely for the risks we took. Not to mention the innocent lives we saved.

That was enough for me. Let politicians be the slimeballs they typically were, so long as my conscious was clean and I felt like I was doing the right thing. But lately Tory had wanted more.

She'd begun talking about moving to privatized services and had even begun making contacts in some underground sectors for black-ops contractors. Mercenaries for hire, or worse.

"We're putting our necks out for pennies when we could be doing half the work for three times the pay."

"Tory, you're asking me to betray my country, my unit, just for an easy payday."

"Si..come on, you know the minute we leave these weapons are just going to go right back into the hands of the people we're trying to keep them from. We're just wasting our time, our blood and sweat, and tears for nothing. None of this matters in the end. We're just the pawns on their fucking chessboard. The most expendable pieces they have to play." Her blue eyes pleaded with mine to believe her, to join her.

Pain arched from the soles of my feet and I snapped back to the present.

"You seem to have drifted away there, Simon." Sybil's eyes glinted in the dimness of the room, a predator watching her prey. "You were just telling me how Tory's death was my fault."

"You, you killed her. You sold her a lie and it killed her."

Suddenly, nails like knives sank into the lacerations that crisscrossed my abdomen and I did cry out in pain this time. My back and neck arched as the breath was snatched away from me and I was left gasping for air. Darkness clouded the edges of my vision and as I began to fade out of consciousness I felt her hot breath against my ear. "Tory knew exactly what she was getting into, if anything I gave her the chance to free herself from a life of lies. If anyone's lying, it's you, Simon.

Don't try to twist the truth, I'm not the one with her blood on my hands, isn't that right... *Reaper.*"

CHAPTER TWO

Hannah

I looked down at the shiny black pumps on my feet and watched as if from a distance as they tapped a fast rhythm on the white and pristine marbled floor. The marble was so shiny I could just make out the red reflection of their bottoms. Whenever I felt I needed a little extra boost of confidence I always went to my Louboutin's and if ever I needed that boost, it was today. Shifting in the stiff leather chair I sighed and glanced up at the large clock on the wall just across from me. They say justice is patient, but somehow I must have missed that memo. Because all I could think was that with every tick of the clock the seconds were eating at the distance between me and my sister.

I felt a presence next to me like a dark shadow but I didn't turn toward it. Ever since I'd agreed to help Rue locate Simon, either she, Micheal, or Evan had been a constant presence at my side. They'd insisted it was for my protection since the Abromov Group, or rather Sybil, would be targeting me, but it felt more like they were making sure I didn't back out of my end of the bargain.

And the bargain? I'd find Sybil and in turn, locate Simon, but then Sybil was mine to deal with. They would get what they needed to shut down the weapons dealing portion of the

Abromov Group, but I'd get my sister. And then I'd get my justice.

But first, I had to piece back together the shambles of my life that Sybil had destroyed. Starting with getting reinstated as an FBI agent and clearing my name.

Rubbing sweaty palms on the front of my slacks I finally turned to look at the large figure who was leveling me with his dark gaze. I'd thought Micheal and I had come to an understanding when we were in Switzerland, or at least, an easy comradery. But since the night at the gala, he'd been back to silently promising to kill me a hundred different ways with just a look.

It pissed me off.

What right did he have to be upset with me? He and the rest of the team had been just as guilty as Simon when they'd lied about their true intentions. But now he acted as if I was the enemy and he was just waiting for the chance to dump me off in the nearest ditch.

I stared right back at him and then slowly as if I was pulling something from the pocket of my suit jacket, flipped him off. I could see the vein in his temple pulse as he visibly tensed and I thought for a second he was finally going to unleash all that pent-up rage on me.

"Ms. Kelly."

Startled I looked up at a stout middle-aged woman who had just opened the office door across the hall from where Michael and I were waiting. She cleared her throat and pushed bright purple framed glasses up her broad face while casting a nervous glance towards Micheal.

"Yous?" I squeaked out, quickly hiding my hand back in the pocket of my jacket. I didn't dare look over at Michael but could feel his satisfied smirk burning a hole in my head.

"They're ready for you now, ma'am."

I sighed and stood, casting one last glance down to my lucky shoes, and then touched the Saint Micheal pendant that always hung around my neck, sending up a silent prayer to the patron saint of law enforcement. If I'd had a four-leaf clover or rabbit's foot I'd probably have touched those too, but so far Saint Micheal and Louboutin had never failed me. I was counting on that now. Then I followed the secretary through the door, leaving Micheal to wait for me in the lobby.

When I entered the conference room the secretary ushered me towards I felt my nerves settle like a ball of lead in my gut. David sat on one side of the large table next to two other people, one man, and one woman. I scanned his face trying to pick up on any subtle cues or hints he may give me about how the hearing had gone but his face was impassive.

Directly to David's left, sat a man I'd hoped to never have to meet. Assistant Director of the Office of Professional Responsibility Frank Reed was a thin man with a slightly receding hairline of light brown hair. His office was directly in charge of internal investigations of FBI agents and field offices. I was slightly surprised to see him in the seat next to David though, or even in this office. Normally the OPR sent their own investigators to dig up the dirt on agents under suspicion of misconduct. I swallowed past the lump in my throat. Maybe my charms had finally worn out their luck.

To Assistant Director Reed's left was a stern-looking blonde woman I'd only see glimpses of in hiring announcements or news bulletins. Angela Waters, Executive Assistant Director of the intelligence branch of the FBI. I could understand why Agent Reed was here, but to have the Executive Assistant for all of FBI Intelligence in the room overseeing my reinstatement hearing baffled me.

I paused in front of the table and tried to present myself as the professional and dedicated special agent that I was. Because ultimately it didn't matter why they were in this room, I had one goal today and that was to begin unraveling the fucking mess my sister had made of my life.

"Senior Special Agent Hannah Kelly, thank you for joining us." Agent Reed began first and motioned for me to take the chair directly across from him.

"Thank you for having me sir," I looked from him to Agent Waters, "Ma'am."

My Memaw used to say, "You can't make a silk purse out of a sow's ear." Which basically meant, you shouldn't expect to get something from nothing. She also used to say that about her neighbor Mrs. Billings who she was always feuding with but I think that meant something entirely different then. For now, though, I used the phrase to mean that if I wanted this meeting to go in the direction I needed it to, I would have to be on my best behavior. And maybe lay on the southern charm just a little thick.

Reed cleared his throat and tapped the thick manila envelope on the table in front of him. "Agent Kelly, I don't think I need to tell you how serious these accusations are that are brought against you. But after some serious discussion with Agent Williams and the evidence you brought forward along with the sworn statements of your friends, I have decided that there can only be two outcomes to this hearing."

"They aren't my friends." The words were out of my mouth before I could blink and instantly winced in regret, especially when I saw Agent Waters arch one manicured eyebrow in intrigue.

"Pardon?" Agent Reed didn't look amused and cleared his throat again. I was beginning to wonder if it was a tick he had or if he genuinely needed a cough drop.

"I just mean that Ethan and Micheal aren't my friends." I was careful not to mention Rue given her history with the bureau. "I wouldn't even consider them colleagues. And while I appreciate that they wrote statements verifying my account and Sybil's involvement in framing me, I do not feel that I owe them any debt of friendship, or that they reciprocate it." A little tug of sadness whispered through me. At one point I had begun to consider them friends. But now? I couldn't trust them and if there was one lesson my sister had taught me over and over, was to not trust the people who were supposed to be there for you.

He cleared his throat again, and now I was sure it was some nervous tick, as he leaned back in his chair and looked first to Agent Waters and then to David. I wasn't sure what the silent exchange was meant to convey but I had the suspicion that it was confirming a conversation I hadn't been privy to.

"And yet you've agreed to continue to work with them in order to locate their missing team leader." This time it was the husky voice of Agent Waters that I turned towards. Her cold gaze studied me intensely. I had the eerie feeling that I was being examined from the inside out. It was similar to the way Simon had analyzed me. As if he could read every thought. Only with Simon, I found myself wanting to open up to him. To show him every dark corner and the secret thing I'd hidden away. Agent Waters, on the other hand, had me running to all my dirty closet doors and slamming them firmly shut. Somehow I didn't think it would help though.

"No ma'am. I did not agree to work with them to find Mr. Gallagher." I expected her to object to my statement but she didn't flinch or speak, just waited for me to continue. "I couldn't give two shits what happens to Simon. I agreed to help them, and to ask your permission to do so, in order to find Sybil and bring her back to answer for her crimes."

Reed cleared his throat again and I wondered how rude it would be if I offered him a cough drop from my purse. "You ask our permission now, but you didn't think to ask our permission when you went gallivanting off to Stockholm while you were under criminal investigation from the O.P.R.?"

I resisted the urge to squirm in my seat under the intense scrutiny from my three superiors across from me. That had probably been the hardest and most difficult conversation I'd ever had with David. When I'd gotten back from Stockholm and had filled him in on everything that happened he'd looked at me with such disappointment that it felt like I was a kid getting scolded by my dad again.

"Hannah, how could you do something so stupid?"
"David I didn't have a choice."
"Wrong Hannah, there is always a choice. Always."

"I understand that what I did was and could be considered a conflict of interest. But I assure you, I had no intention of violating the trust of my superiors or my government. I was blinded by grief and made some poor decisions based on limited information." I swallowed and raised my chin a notch. Trusting the word of a Ghost and not going directly to my superior, David, with the information I had was foolish. But like everything that involved Sybil, I rushed headlong into the danger before even thinking about how it would affect me. White-hot rage flared through me. Even then, when she was supposed to have been dead, she'd been manipulating me. Controlling me. But it was still my decision to run off on a half-cocked mission without the bureau's stamp of approval. The blame could only fall squarely at my feet.

"And I am prepared to face the consequences of those decisions, I only ask that you allow me to rectify what I can and to retrieve the stolen evidence in the Hildago case and to bring my sister back to the U.S. to face justice." I held my breath, meeting the cold gazes of the three people who were going to decide my fate. I could only see this going one of three ways. Either they reinstated me as an agent and let me go back to my job, they fired me and I would be charged with criminal conflict of interest, or they gave me a reprieve to hunt Sybil like I wanted. But Agent Reed had said he could only see two outcomes from this meeting and now I wasn't so sure I knew my future after all.

Continue Reading the second book in the series on Amazon or in Kindle Unlimited today!

Made in the USA
Middletown, DE
26 August 2023